The Pathless Woods

**Ernest Hemingway's
Sixteenth Summer in
Northern Michigan**

Printed in the United States of America

5 4 3 2 1   02 01 00 99

ISBN 1-882376-63-3

Library of Congress Catalog Card Number 98-61302

Cover illustration and design by Glenn Wolff

Center insert photos courtesy of the John F. Kennedy Library, Boston

Holt, Michigan

For my son, Joe,
who knows and loves the
pathless woods of northern Michigan.

There is a pleasure in the pathless woods,
There is a rapture on the lonely shore,
There is society, where none intrudes,
By the deep sea, and music in its roar:
I love not man the less, but Nature more.

Childe Harold's Pilgrimage
George Noel Gordon, Lord Byron

Author's Note

How do you tell the story of someone's life when it is not your life? Ernest Hemingway's brother, Leicester, and his sisters, Madelaine and Marcelline, wrote books about their brother. There are still people living in northern Michigan who remember him. Windemere, the Hemingway cottage, still stands on the shore of Walloon Lake. The blue water and the green hills are there still. When I wrote the book I found dusty copies of the Charlevoix *Courier* for 1915 piled in the basement of the Charlevoix library. Some of the stories Ernest Hemingway wrote are about his childhood on Walloon Lake.

All of these things helped make this imagined life of Ernest Hemingway, and so did my own memories of what it is like to be young in northern Michigan in the summertime.

Thunder Bay Press Titles
by Gloria Whelan
Friends

Other Books by Gloria Whelan
A Time to Keep Silent
The Indian School
Next Spring an Oriole
Night of the Full Moon
Once on This Island
Shadow of the Wolf
That Wild Berries Should Grow

Contents

1

Return to Longfield Farm

Ernie pulled the boat well up on the beach. When he finished unloading his camping gear, he stood looking across Walloon Lake at his family's summer cottage, wondering what his mother and sisters were doing. In one way or another he was moving farther away from his family. He didn't know why. He liked them all a lot. The separation had begun last year when he had talked his father into letting him camp out in a tent all summer at Longfield Farm. It wasn't really a farm. It was just some acreage his dad had bought so he would have a place to put in fruit trees and a vegetable garden. Ernie liked it because of its isolation and its rolling hills and the view he had from his tent of the long blue lake.

His father approved of Ernie being on his own in the woods. "Nature is the best school there is," he told Ernie. His dad thought you ought to be learning things every minute. If you weren't, you were wasting your time. Ernie was glad to know most of the things his dad taught him:

how to clean a fish so you could pull its guts right out of its gill and leave it whole, and then how to skin and bone it so you had two smooth, pearly white filets. He even showed Ernie how to make bullets from the mold Ernie's grandfather had brought back from the Civil War. When his grandfather gave Ernie a single-barrel twenty-gauge shotgun for his birthday, his dad taught him how to keep it clean and oiled and how to carry it through the woods and over fences so you didn't have an accident. He never allowed Ernie more than three slugs of ammunition for the gun at one time. "That'll teach you to make each shot count," he said.

Ernie knew he ought to drag his gear up to his camp-site next to the spring and pitch his tent. The June sky had stayed light about as long as it was going to. If his father were with him, the tent would be up by now. You didn't sit around on your fanny when his dad was there. His dad didn't even like to see him reading. "Put your book down and do something useful," he'd tell Ernie.

Ernie decided to rest for a minute. He had done plenty of work this past week. Four days ago when the horse and dray arrived at their house in the Chicago suburb of Oak Park, his dad was at the hospital operating on some-one. That left Ernie with the job of loading the trunks and boxes that were to go to Windemere, their summer place on Walloon Lake. His mother and sisters weren't much help, except for Sunny. She was only eleven, but she had more guts than all the rest of his sisters put together. She tried to move packages that were nearly as big as she was, lugging them around in her skinny arms.

The family took a streetcar from their big three-story house on Kenilworth Street to the pier on Lake Michigan, where they boarded the steamer *Manitou.* For Ernie, the most exciting moment of the trip was when he stood on the deck of the *Manitou* and watched the Chicago skyline disappear, knowing he was on the way to the woods of northern Michigan. It was at exactly that moment that he could forget about being Ernest Hemingway: high school sophomore, football player, boxer, cellist, glee club member, debater, and member of the hiking club and the Christian Endeavor Society. He just became Ernie, someone he liked better. In Oak Park he was always worrying about what his friends thought of him. At Walloon Lake he could be himself.

After the three-day steamer voyage along the coast of Lake Michigan, the *Manitou* docked at the small resort town of Harbor Springs. From there the Hemingways went by railroad to the larger town of Petoskey. The rhythmic jerking of the train was different from the rocking glide of the steamer. There was so much stop and start to it that it made Ernie impatient. Neither the steamer nor the train could keep pace with the way his thoughts raced ahead to Walloon Lake and Windemere. It seemed to take forever to chug past the rows of wooden cottages painted in summer colors and trimmed with carpenters' lace. The resorters had strung their summer homes along the railroad because the railroad was their lifeline back to the city. Ernie was happy his parents hadn't been afraid to build their summer place off by itself.

Coming into Petoskey that morning, everyone on the train was talking about the fire in the Arlington Hotel the night before. Fanned by strong winds, flames destroyed the huge hotel in less than two hours. As the train passed the blackened hull, the passengers grew silent. With the woods coming right up to the backs of the cottages, fire was always a threat.

The Arlington had stood on a bluff overlooking Lake Michigan. For years Ernie and his sisters had competed with one another to see who would be the first to spot the hotel from the railing of the *Manitou.* The sight of the famous inn meant their trip was nearly over. It had been one of the fanciest hotels in northern Michigan and actually had running water and electric lights in every room.

From Petoskey a smaller railway took them to Walloon Lake, where a launch carried them across the lake to Windemere. His mother had named their cottage after a place she had read about in England that had something to do with a poet. It was a pretty fancy name for the small, white clapboard house. With the first glimpse of the cottage, Ernie's memories of all the summers he had spent there crowded in on him and he couldn't see why he ever had to go back to Oak Park.

This summer, because his dad remained behind in Chicago to deliver a crop of babies, Ernie hadn't been able to escape to Longfield Farm right away. Instead he had spent the day helping his mother and sisters at the cottage, getting in firewood for the stove, priming the pump, and taking down the shutters. Summer seemed to start when you got the shutters off and looked out through the opened eyes of the windows to the maple trees, the big blue lake, and the hills beyond it.

His younger sisters, Ursula, Carol, and Sunny, unpacked the provisions, hunting for the ginger snaps and hard candies among the piles of boxes. His older sister, Marcelline, went around with a broom and dustpan and a disgusted look, cleaning up the mouse dirt that had accumulated all winter. His mother, who always managed to avoid the housework, was busy trying to settle Ernie's new baby brother, Leicester, who was only three months old. Ernie hadn't been much older than that when he had first come to Windemere. This would be his sixteenth summer.

Early in the evening they had all sat down to a dinner of thick slices of smoked ham and cold potato salad made the way he liked it, with lots of vinegar and pieces of onion and bacon. For dessert there were some of his father's preserved blueberries left over from the summer before. Camping out he'd miss all that good food—except for what Sunny might smuggle over to him in exchange for Ernie letting her hang around his camp.

After dinner he and Sunny had gone out to sit on the dock. He never minded having her tag along because she knew when to shut up. They took off their shoes and socks and tried to see who could get their bare feet closest to the surface of the water without touching it. The water was still cold from the memory of the winter ice. A school of perch flicked in and out of a weedbed. Ernie considered catching a few, but the big dinner had made him lazy and he didn't want to move out of the sun. Even that late in the day it was warm and comforting on his back.

They hadn't been sitting there more than five minutes when Marce appeared to tell him his mother had found the hole where the mice were getting in and would he *please* come and do something about it *right* away.

He liked Marcelline. She was pretty. But in the past year they stopped being good friends and were just brother and sister. Marce was dating now and even though she was only a year older than he was, she considered herself an adult and him a child. And she let him know it. The worst thing was that for a long time she had been a whole head taller than he was. He had caught up to her now, but he still couldn't forgive her for those years she had towered over him. She was his mother's favorite, too, and his mother was always holding her up to Ernie's other sisters as an example of how to be a proper young lady.

It had been nearly dark before he had finally been able to escape in the boat and row across the lake to Longfield Farm. Now he stood on the beach of Longfield, relieved to be by himself. Looking out over the lake to the distant hills, he tried to picture how it had been twenty years before when the whole countryside was covered with giant white pine trees. The shade from those great trees had been so dense that nothing could grow in the woods and you could look down the long aisles between the trees for a mile or more. If he didn't want to be seen, a man moving along one of those forest aisles could steal slyly from one great pine to another. He would have to put his feet down softly on a bed of dry pine needles to move silently enough to keep a crow or a squirrel from starting up and giving him away. Indians could walk that way. They still did. When Ernie walked with his friend, Ted Lacour, and Ted's sister, Nina, who were part Indian and part French, Ted and Nina would walk though the woods without making a sound, while Ernie tramped along making all kinds of noise no matter how quiet he tried to be.

Nearly all the virgin pine was gone now. There was still one small sawmill on the lake but in a year or so only the big hemlocks would be left, and even they were going fast. He had noticed the inroads the Indians had made on the trees since he had been there last fall. They cut the hemlocks down for bark and sold the bark to the tannery in Boyne City.

With the deep shade of the big pines gone, young maple and beech and poplar trees were springing up. The deer were increasing. Last summer Ernie had seen deer in the early morning and the early evening drinking at the spring near his tent.

There was only a faint suggestion of light over the western hills where the sun had been. Across the lake someone had lit the oil lamps at Windemere. The lighted windows seemed far away. Off in the distance he heard a loon cry. It was not the call of the male to the female nor the wolf cry; it was the shrill wail a desperate loon sends out when it is in danger. Looking out at the darkening lake and the soft yellow glow from the cottage windows made Ernie feel how alone he was. Camping here he cut himself off from the rest of the family. They were such a close family, too close sometimes. In Oak Park he had to live his life without the pleasure of secrets.

He made his way up the hill to his old campsite. It wouldn't take him long to pitch his tent. Last fall he had left everything in good order. The ridge pole and stakes had been neatly stashed away. The camp stove that he made from big chunks of fieldstone would be there. He was coming home. The house in Oak Park, even Windemere, belonged to his parents. This was his own place.

The path up the hill was steep and the straps from his duffel bag cut into his shoulders. The backs of his legs were aching. I'm out of shape, he thought, and he was planning the long hikes he would take to toughen up when he stumbled over a small boulder. He knew every inch of the trail from the beach to the camping site. He had climbed it a thousand times last summer. There were no boulders on the beach. A few steps farther he came upon a second one. There was something else, the smell of wood burning.

He hurried toward his campsite, his duffel bag bumping against his back. The shapes of the two big stones were familiar. He reached the clearing where he had pitched his tent last year. Ashes and bits of charred wood lay scattered about. Someone had made a fire of his ridge-pole and stakes. One blackened end of the pole and a single stake lay among the ashes. The stake was still burning. Heat was rising from the ashes. Whoever had done it had known the Hemingways were back and that Ernie would be coming over to the camp that night. The stones from his stove had been pushed down the hill. The three-legged camp stool he had fashioned from a maple burl and lovingly polished had been chopped into bits.

Everything was spoiled for him. All winter long, whenever something disappointed him or things had gone wrong, he would think about Longfield. He would close his eyes and see his campsite waiting for him just as he had left it. Now it was wrecked.

For a moment he thought he should return to Windemere and spend the night there. But if he did there would have to be explanations. His mother would know something was wrong. She liked to keep an eye on him and without his dad there to stick up for him she would put an end to his camping out.

It was too dark to prepare a new site. Ernie hunted through his gear for his hatchet and cut some feathery hemlock branches to sleep on. Without bothering to take off his clothes he rolled himself up in a blanket. He could hear the small tongues of waves lapping at the shore down on the beach. They had a greedy sound, as if they were eating closer and closer to him. Only a few feet from his head, the spring made friendly splashing sounds on its way over the pebbles to the lake below. A loon shrieked. He wondered what was frightening it. Maybe a fox was padding near the loon's nest. It wasn't a sound he liked to hear when he was alone. His anger slid into a kind of panic. What sort of person would purposely do all that damage? And where was he now?

As Ernie's eyes grew accustomed to the dark he saw one star appear after another. He tried to forget what had happened by staring at an empty stretch of sky and waiting for it to fill up with stars. Then he concentrated on another stretch. After a while the whole heavens were filled up. It made him feel like he had something to do with it. He had read in a science article in one of his *St. Nicholas* magazines that some of the stars you saw in the sky had burned up thousands of years before but it took that long for the light to reach you. No wonder the light was so cold. He counted 1,306 stars before he fell asleep.

Once during the night he awoke. He was dreaming of footsteps and shafts of light and whispers. He sat up. The loon was calling. Probably it was the loon's cry that had awakened him. He burrowed back down into the fragrance of the hemlock boughs where sleep was waiting for him.

2

Death of a Porcupine

He awoke to the screech of sea gulls rotating crazily over his head. When they migrated inland from Lake Michigan in large numbers like that, it usually meant rain. He knew he ought to strip and get washed in the lake but the sky was clouding over. There would be no sun to warm him. If his dad were there they would have gone in anyway. He scooped some water out of the spring and splashed it on his face, feeling ashamed of his lack of willpower. But in a minute he changed his mind. Perhaps it was the feeling he often had that his father was looking over his shoulder, judging him. Being weak led to being a coward, and being a coward, Ernie believed, was about the worst thing that could happen to you. He grabbed a towel and ran down the hill and along the beach, working up a sweat before he plunged into the cold water like the Finn lumberjacks used to do. He was heading for a small cove where a spit of sand stretched out into the lake. You walked out on the spit, the sand firm under your feet, and then there was a sudden drop-off. You only had to take one step and you were swimming without the torture of slowly immersing yourself in the cold water.

The spit had built up over the years as a small creek that emptied into the lake left behind deposits of sand. Hemlock and cedar grew along the edge of the stream. You could find watercress there for sandwiches and wild mint that made good tea. Deer often came to graze on the watercress beds. Their heart-shaped tracks were all around, clear and sharp in the damp sand. Once he had camped there overnight. He remembered the smell of the mint as he fell asleep and how he awakened in the morning to see a big buck about twenty yards from him pulling up the watercress, the herb's long roots dangling from his chin like a green beard.

When he reached the stream he was not surprised to find deer tracks. What was surprising were the footprints that intermingled with the tracks, lots of them. Prints from two or three different-sized boots.

Ernie remembered his dream of the night before, dreams of footsteps and whispers. Probably someone doing a little night fishing. The bass were on their nests now. It was against the law, but you could spot them with a flashlight in the shallows.

He pulled off his clothes and waded out on the spit of sand, talking himself into what was coming. The icy water touched his legs. He reached the drop-off and took a deep breath. The next minute water closed over him, numbing his body.

He swam out about a quarter of a mile and back in again. He imagined he was the great English poet, Lord Byron, swimming the Hellespont in Turkey. Byron was his hero. He was not only a great poet but he had fought for the freedom of Italy and Greece. The water began to feel warm but the minute the morning air hit him he started to shiver. He dried himself off with the towel, rubbing hard to get his circulation going, pleased that he hadn't given in to his laziness.

The sky was developing the thick, blotchy look of a bowl of cooked oatmeal. He decided he'd better get his tent up fast. Rain was coming. He raced back to his camp. There'd be hell to pay if he let his books from the Oak Park Library get wet. He had brought up *The Deerslayer* by James Fenimore Cooper, lots of Scott's novels, and Theodore Roosevelt's book about game hunting in Africa. When his dad saw the stack of books he shook his head and grumbled about weeds taking over the vegetable garden while Ernie wore out his eyes and the seat of his pants. But Ernie took the books along anyhow. There wasn't anything better than sitting in his tent with a book while the rain made little plopping noises on the canvas.

The spot he chose to pitch his tent had a fine view of Walloon. The soil was sandy and carried away any rainwater. It was not too close to the hemlock trees, so there was no danger of a campfire singeing the green boughs. It was open enough so that the sun dried the dew off the tent.

He paced off the dimensions, stopping to chuck away

four or five rocks scattered there by whoever wrecked his camp stove. Just let them try that kind of stuff again while he was there. Next he carefully dug a trench around the tent site, making a straight cut about four inches down into the sandy soil. He cut three poplar saplings, pounded two of them well into the ground, and then cut out their center trunks about five feet up to make a crotch. He laid the third sapling between the two Ys and nailed it down. Where the back of the tent would go, he whittled four new stakes with his hatchet and drove them in for the guy ropes. He walked back into the woods and returned with a heavy log to weigh the ropes down.

When the tent was raised and his cot set up, he cut two more saplings to pound in at either corner of the inside of the tent. A third sapling went across the forked stakes. On this he hung his pack with his clothes and books. Two shorter forked stakes were pounded in to support his shotgun. When he was finished he took one of the books out of his pack and lay down on his cot, sure that even his father would approve of the efficient way he had gone about setting things up. Later on he would build a new fireplace and a latrine. For now there would be the luxury of just lying there and reading as long as he pleased.

He opened *African Game Trails* by Theodore Roosevelt. The book was full of pictures of lions and rhinos and elephants. There were illustrations of Roosevelt's campsites, too. It wasn't hard to imagine that his own tent was somewhere in the African bush. That was the great thing about tents. There wasn't anywhere in the world you couldn't go if you had a tent. When you wanted to move on, you just packed up your tent.

He read how Colonel Roosevelt crept through tall grass after a lion he had wounded. If he were in the same situation, Ernie wondered if he would be brave enough to stalk an injured lion, knowing at any second it might jump out at him. The swish of the wind through the hemlock trees became wind stirring tall African grasses. The screech of the gulls was the rasping call of buzzards waiting to see if they were going to pick the bones of a dead lion or a dead man. He had just sighted the sinuous form of the lion ready to pounce on him and was raising his Winchester 405 when he heard his name followed by the family call sounding over the water: "Ooohta-oohta-oohta-ha!"

The African veldt disappeared. He saw his sister Sunny rowing across the lake toward him. She looked small sitting in the boat but she was pretty good with the oars. He returned the call and started down to the lake.

Sunny beached the boat and ran toward him. She was wearing denim overalls and a sweater. Her blond hair was parted in the center and pulled back with a blue ribbon the exact color of her eyes. She had shot up this last year and her long legs and arms gave her the incomplete look of a puppy whose ears and paws are too big for its small body. But one day, he thought, she'd be a good-looking woman. Even now she had great legs.

"Ernie, you've got to bring your gun and come back with me to the cottage," she called to him, excited at being the one to deliver the news. "A porcupine woke everybody up about four o'clock this morning. It was chewing on the cabin and it sounded like the whole place was going to come apart. You can see all his teeth marks and there's a big hunk out of the corner of the cottage. Mother says come and shoot it or we won't have any house left. Here, I brought you these." Sunny handed him two slightly mangled corn muffins.

He hadn't made any breakfast for himself and the muffins tasted good.

"You can come on up while I get my gun," he told her.

She was already on her way up to the tent. This spring he had heard her begging his father to let her camp out for the summer, too. His father wavered but his mother said a firm no. "How can you expect these girls to manage households one day when you encourage them to run wild?" she complained.

"Ernie," Sunny said, "remember that porcupine you shot in the woods last year when the Bacons' dog got a face full of quills and Dad made you eat it?"

Dr. Hemingway didn't approve of shooting animals unless they were destroying property or were going to be used for food. The porcupine had been an old one and even after a lot of cooking, plenty chewy. Ernie changed the subject. "What's happening at the cottage?" he asked.

"Just the usual stuff. Marce says if she can't have a room all to herself she'll go back to Oak Park. She says we get into her things. Mother made Ursula take cod liver oil because she was coming down with a cold and that made her sick to her stomach and she wouldn't eat any breakfast. Carol slammed her toe in the screen door. Leicester's cutting a tooth. And Mother started out playing her Caruso opera records at eight o'clock in the morning. Why can't I come and stay with you? I'd keep the tent clean for you and wash your socks."

"I don't wear socks in the summer."

"I could do your cooking, only you'd have to show me how first."

"Yeah, like that toffee you made last year." Sunny had mistaken the salt for sugar. He saw that he had hurt her feelings. "Maybe you can spend a night here later in the summer," he told her.

"That's a promise, Ernie. Will you spit on it?" They both spit on the ground.

She began rummaging around in his duffel bag. "How come you brought a razor when you don't have to shave yet?"

"Get out of there. What I bring is my own business. Anyhow, I might have to before the summer's over."

"Is it true Indians don't have beards?"

"Sure."

"Well, how come Mr. Lacour has one?"

"Because he's part French."

"I wish I were part Indian. Are you still sweet on Nina Lacour?"

"Shut up and let's go." He had found himself thinking about Nina plenty since he had been back. About her thick black hair and her brown doe's eyes that were quick and shy and startled-looking when she caught you staring at her. He picked up his gun and counted out two slugs of ammunition. "That should be more than enough for a porcupine. The stupid things don't even move when you go after them."

"Can I help you row?" Sunny asked.

"No, our strokes don't match. The boat'll keep turning. You were doing a good job this morning, though. I watched you."

Pleased, Sunny settled down in the back of the boat. "I'll hold your gun so it doesn't get wet on the bottom of the boat. I remember how you said to hold it."

He liked to row. He practiced moving the oars soundlessly through the water. In *The Deerslayer,* Hawkeye and his Indian friend Chingaychgook could move over the water without making a sound. He thought their lake, Glimmerglass, must have been a lot like Walloon, only more wild. As they approached the shore Ernie glanced furtively around. He was at Glimmerglass where Indians from a hostile tribe were watching from behind the trees.

"What have you got that funny look on your face for, Ernie?"

"Keep quiet and help me get the boat tied up."

"We found the porcupine," Carol called out.

"We chased it up the birch tree next to the wood-pile," Ursula told them. "Marce is keeping an eye on it from the kitchen window."

He took his gun and walked toward the woodpile, the three girls trailing after him. He wasn't too thrilled about shooting a porcupine. It was about as exciting as shooting a stone. He could see it about halfway up the tree, its fat body rolled in a ball. He thought with envy of Theodore Roosevelt going after lions. The three girls were standing behind him waiting expectantly. Marce and his mother were watching from the kitchen window. They probably weren't thinking about lions. Maybe his shooting the porcupine would impress them. He threw the bolt and aimed carefully. A second after he pulled the trigger the porcupine fell out of the tree and landed with a dull thud on the ground.

He had a sinking feeling when he looked at the dead porcupine. It was a feeling he always got when he killed an animal. He liked to hunt but he felt a sort of bond between himself and his victim. It was hard to put it into words. He almost loved the animal he was hunting and he was sorry he had to kill it. At least his father wasn't here and he wouldn't have to eat it.

The girls ran over to the porcupine and gingerly tested the sharpness of its quills with their fingers. Marce had come out of the kitchen and his mother was right behind her. "You're as good a shot as your father, Ernie," his mother said. He was pleased although he knew she was just trying to be nice. It wasn't true. His father was the best shot he'd ever seen. Partly because his eyes were so good. He could count every feather in a crow's wing. Ernie's own eyesight wasn't nearly that accurate, especially since he had injured his eye boxing in school.

"Let's give the hunter a good lunch," his mother said. "Come on, girls, get the table set."

A fine rain began to fall and all the girls followed Mrs. Hemingway except Sunny, who was poking at the porcupine with a stick. "Maybe we should take the porcupine over to the Indian camp," she said. "You could give it to Nina and she'd make you one of those fancy porcupine quill boxes." Sunny didn't see why Ernie was so stuck on Nina.

"Come on in the house before you get wet and and shrink some more," he told her. He thought about the rain falling on his tent and how all his things were safely stored away. He wished he were back there reading the book about Africa with the rain beating down on the canvas. He looked across the lake wondering if he could make some excuse about having to go back to check and see if everything was dry. Before he could think of one, his mother called more insistently and he followed Sunny into the cottage.

After lunch his sisters settled down in front of the fireplace with a deck of cards to play fish. He was on the window seat with his legs stretched out and his feet propped up against the wall. He could hear his mother in the bedroom singing the "Berceuse" from *Joslyn* to Leicester. The lullaby was familiar. He had heard her singing it to Ursula and Sunny and Carol as each new baby had come along. He supposed she had once sung it to him. Her voice was rich and deep and different from her speaking voice. Hearing her sing was like having a mysterious stranger in the house.

Before his mother had married his dad she had taken voice lessons in New York with Madame Cappianni, who was a famous teacher. The Metropolitan Opera Company had offered her a contract to sing with them. She said she turned it down because the spotlights on the stage hurt her eyes. Even now being out in the sun gave her an awful headache. Maybe she had decided against a career because she had been in love with his dad and wanted to get married. He knew there were times when she wished she had signed that contract with the Metropolitan Opera. Sometimes she sat listening to the famous Madame Schumann-Heink's records with a dreamy look on her face. Once she told him, "That woman has the place I might have had, Ernie." It was because of her voice that she didn't mess around with the housework. When she was a little girl her parents made her practice all the time. If she tried to cook or anything, they said, "You're wasting your talent, Grace."

Listening to her croon the tender song to the baby made Ernie restless and faintly irritated. It bothered him that at his age he was still so moved by hearing his mother sing a lullaby. He swung his feet on the floor and sat up. "How about a game of Truth?" he said.

The three younger girls shouted, "Yes!" Marce shrugged, but she put down her cards.

"Who's going to be on the spot?" Ursula asked.

"Ernie," Sunny and Marce said.

He didn't mind. Whoever was "it" was always the center of attention and it was his own game. He had been the one to introduce it to the family. Anyhow, when just the girls were playing they never gave you much of a penalty for not telling the truth.

"Which one of us is the prettiest?" Ursula asked.

"Marce," he answered.

"Which one of us is the smartest?" from Sunny.

"Ursula."

"Who's the nicest?" Marce asked.

"Sunny." Out of the corner of his eye he saw Sunny grin that wide grin of hers and then clap a pillow over her face.

"Who's the ugliest in the whole family?" Carol asked.

"Leicester." For years Ernie had looked forward to having a brother, but what good was a brother when he was only three months old, red-faced and crying?

"Who do you like best, Mother or Dad?" Ursula asked.

He stopped to think. He wasn't afraid his answer would get back to his parents. It was understood among them that anything said during the game stayed an absolute secret. It was just that he wasn't sure how to answer.

His mother was always there. In a way she sort of ran the family. And she was pretty and she wrote down any little thing they did in a special scrapbook she kept about each one of them.

But it was his dad he always tried to be like. His dad had hunted with Indians when he was young and learned some of their secrets. He knew everything about camping out and hunting and fishing. But there was a side to his father he didn't approve of. His father did a lot of the cooking and housekeeping because his mother hated it. When they didn't have a maid, his father got all the meals. He did the canning and preserving too, proudly packing away jars filled with peaches and pears and applesauce and jams and pickles to take back to Oak Park at the end of the summer. Ernie thought that was a dumb thing for a man to do. You'd never catch him doing something like that.

"Come on, who do you like best?" Ursula repeated.

"Mother."

"What was the worst thing you ever had to do?" Sunny wanted to know.

"Take Marce to dancing class at the Colonial Club." You had to wear a stiff collar and bow from the waist when you asked a girl to dance and you *had* to ask them, even if they were ugly. And when he had danced with Marce she had been a head taller than he was.

"Thanks a lot!" Marce said. "Have you ever necked with a girl?" His younger sisters giggled.

Marce was only asking that to get back at him. She knew he hadn't but she also knew he hated to admit it. The only date he had ever had was taking Dorothy Davis to a basketball game. "No," he said and decided when it was Marce's turn he'd get even. He was pretty sure she hadn't necked either.

"What do you like to eat best?" Carol was always thinking about food.

"Wild onion sandwiches."

"Ugh!" Carol said.

"What are you most afraid of?" Sunny asked him.

"Nothing." That wasn't a boast. It was almost true. Sometimes it worried him because not being afraid got you into trouble. You did dumb things. He remembered how once, when he was no older than Carol was now, his dad took him along in the horse and carriage to make a house call on a patient. While his dad was inside, Ernie got out and hitched up the horses and drove down the middle of the road and nearly got himself killed. At the time his dad was furious with him, but later, when his dad thought he wasn't around, he had overheard Dr. Hemingway say proudly, "That Ernie isn't afraid of anything."

"What girl do you like best?" Ursula asked.

He felt his face go red. Nothing was going to make him tell them about Nina Lacour. He didn't care what they made him do. He sat there silent.

"Penalty!" they shouted gleefully at him, "Penalty!

penalty!" The four girls put their arms around one another and went into a huddle. Ursula was pushed forward. "You have to wash out all the baby's dirty diapers!" she said.

He started throwing pillows at them. They threw them back, shouting with laughter. He ran after them and they headed for the bedroom. "Mama, Mama," Marce was calling. "Ernie's coming to help you with the diapers."

When he was back at the camp that night, warm under his Hudson Bay three-stripe blanket with the cold rain beating against the canvas roof of his tent and nothing to see out of his window but darkness, and no sounds, not even the distant shriek of the loon, he thought about Nina Lacour. Nina and her brother, Ted, lived near the Indian camp. Her mother was an Indian but her father was mostly French and had some sort of accent. For a while Mr. Lacour had worked with the Indians as a bark peeler, but then he got sore at someone and quit. No one seemed to know what he did now. If you asked Ted and Nina they just changed the subject.

The Lacours lived in a shack that didn't look large enough to hold all of the family. Beside Mr. and Mrs. Lacour and Ted and Nina there were a younger brother Billy, and a sister, Sue. The outside of the shack had never been painted and the boards had weathered to a dark silver gray. Pieces of wood covered broken panes of glass in the windows. The stovepipe leaned to one side. Half the family's belongings seemed strewn about the yard:

broken toys, an old mattress, pails, a washtub, and under a half-dead apple tree, a wooden table and some chairs as though mealtimes at the Lacours' were always picnics. In back of the house the Lacours' old horse nibbled the sparse grass or stood looking off to the green hills it would never travel.

Once when Ernie had gone to call for Ted he found Billy and Sue hunched up behind the trunk of a big maple tree. Loud, angry voices were coming out of the Lacours' shack. It didn't sound like the kind of argument Ernie's own parents had, with his father's voice quiet and firm and his mother's voice righteous and complaining. These voices were vicious and threatening, as though the words were not the argument itself, but just leading up to it. Embarrassed, Ernie had hurried away.

It was hard to imagine Nina being part of a family like that. She was shy and quiet, deferring in everything to her older brother, Ted. Ernie was used to girls like his own sisters who talked all the time and said what they pleased so you knew just what they were thinking. With Nina you never knew. That was one of the reasons he found her so intriguing. He spent a lot of time trying to figure people out. It was important to him to know what they were thinking. It seemed wonderful to him that everyone was wrapped up in their own skin and different from anyone else.

Another thing about Nina. She knew just about everything there was to know about the woods. She could tell you where the burrows of the foxes were and the rabbit warrens and where to see flying squirrels at night. She moved so quietly through the woods that the animals accepted her as one of themselves.

Ernie wished he had been born an Indian and had lived a hundred years ago before Indians wore flannel shirts and overalls and sat on the porch of the Horton Bay Store and gabbed about how many cows got killed by the Pere Marquette railroad.

He imagined himself and another warrior, Wolf Heart (he would be Little Bear) racing their fragile birchbark canoes through a whitewater rapids littered with sharp rocks. The one who won the race would marry Nina, who was the chief's daughter. Her name was Golden Dawn and she dressed in soft white buckskin with a beaded band around her forehead and a single eagle feather in her dark hair because she was a chief's daughter. As he was guiding his canoe through treacherous water toward a whirlpool, Wolf Heart well behind, Ernie fell into a deep sleep where some other, darker part of his mind took over his dreams. The sound of the rain pelting the small early summer leaves and striking the hard sand drowned out the footsteps of the figure who paused for a minute outside Ernie's tent and then moved on into the woods, a single shadow melting into other shadows.

3
Nina

In Oak Park spring came early, easing you into summer. In northern Michigan there was hardly any spring at all. It was cold for longer than you could stand it. Then, when you had just about given up, summer swooped in. While Ernie slept the rain changed from a chilling drizzle to a warm, steamy mist, turning everything it touched green. By midmorning a vigorous sun burned away the mist and the first day of summer arrived. The bluejays were gone. They had perched in the trees next to his tent making noises like rusty hinges and swooping boldly down after bread crumbs. Now they were hushed and quiet, going about their secret summer business of nesting.

It was so warm that Ernie shed his sweater and kicked off his shoes before setting off for the Bacons' farm. It was his first visit of the year to the farm. He always felt at home with Mr. and Mrs. Bacon and their six children. One of the boys, Carl, was his age and a good friend. When they were younger they had taken turns jumping into the haystack and playing hide-and-seek in the corn shucks. The last couple of years they hadn't been as close. Carl was expected to do a man's work on the farm and summer was his busiest time.

Mr. Bacon was so skilled a farmer that his fingertips almost pulled things up from the ground. The vegetable garden he started for the Hemingways at Longfield Farm was already sending up feathery carrot tops and green asparagus spears and little green furled flags of spinach and lettuce. The Bacon farm supplied the Hemingways with milk and eggs. Ernie or one of his sisters made the trip to the farm every day through the thick gray maze of beech trees, down into a ravine and up again, and across a meadow to the white clapboard farmhouse and the red barn that always looked Christmassy against the green trees.

The Indian camp was near the farm so Ernie wasn't surprised to see Ted Lacour walking along through the woods, a gun slung over his shoulder. Then he saw Ted's sister, Nina, walking with him. For a minute Ernie considered turning back. But it was too late. Ted was already waving his gun. Ernie felt embarrassed in front of Nina. He was afraid she might guess how much he liked her.

"Hey, Ernie," Ted called. "I'm sure glad it's you and not Tommy Thrake." Tommy Thrake was the game warden's son. A year or two older than Ernie and Ted, he sneaked around in the woods acting as an official spy for his dad. He didn't like resorters. He particularly didn't like the Hemingways because they had talked the Bacons into selling them Longfield Farm. The Thrakes had wanted it for themselves. Thrake didn't like Indians, either. He was jealous because they knew much more about hunting than he did. Every time Tommy Thrake caught someone he felt important. The rest of the time he didn't.

Nina was carrying three fat fox squirrels her brother had shot. She smiled as she held them up by their bushy tails for Ernie to admire. Even though she was half French she tried to stay clear of white people. She knew what they said about Indians—that they were shiftless and drunk all the time. In Charlevoix there were a lot of places where Indians weren't even welcome to show their faces. They were supposed to slink around in the woods except for once a year when they were expected to turn up for some fake Indian powwow and do a war dance.

Of all the white people she knew, the Hemingways were the only ones Nina trusted. Dr. Hemingway often took care of the Indians when they got sick or were injured and he seldom charged them anything. She thought Ernie could almost have been an Indian himself with his dark hair and eyes and his sunburned skin. He knew a lot about the woods and nearly as much about hunting and fishing as her brother. She wasn't afraid of Ernie. With most white people she tried to be as invisible as a partridge staring furtively out from his cover of brown leaves.

"What do you think you're doing?" Ernie called to Ted. "I thought squirrels were out of season."

"Season, hell," Ted said in a disgusted voice. "It's against the law to shoot any kind of squirrel until 1920. Five more years. Anything you try to shoot now is out of season. Can't shoot ducks or rabbits or deer until next fall. Ten dollars for a beaver license and all you get for a skin is a couple of dollars. They even take the fish from us. No nets allowed in Walloon or Pine Lake anymore. And my dad, where's he goin' to make any money this summer? All these years he's caught trout and pike to sell to the restaurants. Now it's against the law. They say Indians don't work. They're shiftless. How can we hunt when everything's against the law?"

Nina stole a glance at Ernie to see what he thought about Ted's angry outburst. When she caught Ernie staring at her she dropped her eyes.

"Well, somebody's fishing out of season," Ernie said. "I saw a lot of tracks where that creek on Longfield empties into the lake. Whoever it was might have been the one who messed up my campsite. I guess they didn't want me around to see them."

Nina looked frightened. Ted was silent for a minute. Then he said, "Must be Thrake or his dad. They're always sticking their nose in other people's business. I'd like to see him try to tell me I can't shoot squirrels, law or no law!"

"Maybe they made the law because there aren't too many squirrels left up here," Ernie said. "You can shoot all the wolves and bobcats you want and get a bounty for them."

"Woves? Bobcats? Where've you seen a wolf or a bobcat around here since they built all the hotels and cottages?"

"Yeah, if they keep putting up summer places, in a couple of years it'll be like Oak Park here. Then we may as well stay home." It never occurred to Ernie that his own family were summer people. He felt as though they belonged.

"I'll tell you what they give us to shoot," Ted said. "Rats, that's what. Five cents a head. I'm not going to shoot any darn rats for five cents. Only one thing," Ted started to laugh. "The township clerk has to count all the darn rats you bring in so they know how much money you get. It'd be worth it just to see how that Mrs. Dealy's face looks when you dump your pile of dead rats on her desk."

Ernie grinned. He had gone with his dad to the township office to pay their taxes. He could just see the rats piled up in front of old Mrs. Dealy with her pinched mouth and fluttery hands and her neat desktop that always had a clean green blotter and a little leather cup with a bouquet of sharpened pencils.

"How's the trout fishing over at Horton Creek?" he asked Ted.

"Water's a little high yet from the spring rain. We'll be getting a caddis hatch one night though. You want me to come over and get you if I hear it's on?"

"Sure." Ernie wanted to say something to Nina, who was looking down at the ground, her thick black hair falling over her face. He tried a few things out in his head: "How've you been Nina?" "Want me to hold those dead squirrels for you?" "You've sure got neat looking legs." Finally he managed to get out, "What are you doing this summer, Nina?"

"I want to get a job. Pa's not working. I tried at the hotels, but they said I wasn't old enough."

"You're not going to get a job at any hotel. They don't hire Indians for waitresses," Ted told her. "I gotta find a job myself. Maybe I'll be a bark peeler like my dad was, only I'd hate to be stuck in one place all summer and never have any time in the woods. I get itchy just like him. When he feels like it he just takes off. He doesn't care what my ma says."

Ernie saw Nina shoot an angry look at her brother. He guessed she didn't like him talking about their ma and pa in front of him.

They heard a rustling noise overhead. A squirrel sat looking down at them, whipping its tail. When Ted raised his gun the squirrel glided to another tree. "You wait here," Ted said over his shoulder to Nina. I"m going to get one more squirrel for the pot. Then we can go home. You want to come, Ernie?"

"I've got to get over to the farm," Ernie said. But when Ted took off after the squirrel, Ernie just stood there. Nina laid the three limp bodies on the ground and settled down on a patch of moss, arranging her skirt modestly over her legs. Ernie sat down beside her. He would have liked to reach over and gently push her hair away from her cheek so he could see her face.

"Ernie," Nina's voice was almost a whisper. "Why do you want to camp out at Longfield? Why don't you stay at the cottage with your family?" She paused as if she were deciding how much more she should say. "Maybe whoever it was who spoiled your camp will come back again and do something really bad." She looked nervously over her shoulder as if she wanted to be sure Ted wasn't within listening distance.

Ernie was pleased that Nina was worrying about him. "They won't do anything now that I'm there. I've got a shotgun," he reassured her, but Nina looked more worried than ever.

Suddenly she jumped up. "I know where there's a hummingbird nest," she said. "You want to see it?" She began running, her black hair streaming out behind her. Ernie ran after her, admiring the graceful motion of her long tan legs and the plump pink soles of her bare feet.

They came out of the woods and stopped at the top of the ravine. Nina signaled him to be quiet, pointing to a twig on a branch of a black cherry tree. The branch was about fifteen feet from the ground but because they were at the tip of the incline it stretched out just below them. A whir of iridescent green rose from the twig, flew straight up into the air, and disappeared. "Look quick," Nina whispered. "We don't want to keep the mother away."

Ernie saw a little cup about the size of a walnut shell fastened to the twig. The outside of the cup was covered over with pale gray-green lichen. Inside there were two tiny white eggs nestled in a cushion made from the down of dandelion seeds.

"You know what holds the nest together?" Nina whispered. "Spider webs." Her voice was full of wonder. They stared down at the toy-sized nest for a whole minute. Then they went careening down the ravine, dodging trees, tripping on roots scratching their legs on briars, and stubbing their toes on rocks hidden in the long grasses. They were shouting and laughing, trying to get away as fast as they could from the closeness they had felt in the minute of looking down at the nest together.

When they reached the bottom they threw themselves down breathless on the grass. Ernie looked over at Nina. Her black hair was spread like a fan around her face Her skirt was up to her knees and her brown legs had a long scratch from a wild raspberry bush. Three tiny droplets of blood were forming. It seemed terrible to Ernie that those legs should have been scratched. Without thinking he reached over and tenderly wiped the blood away.

Nina stared at him and then jumped up. "Ted'll be looking for me," she said and began to scramble back up the ravine.

Ernie watched until she disappeared into the woods. He didn't understand why she had run away so suddenly, but it would have been worse if she had stayed. How had he let himself get into a situation where he felt so dumb? So much out of control? He decided he would keep away from Nina, even if it meant not going fishing or hunting with Ted. His dad had warned him not to get involved with girls. "Plenty of time for that, Ernie," he had said. "Keep you mind on your schoolwork." His dad wanted him to be a doctor like he was. But Ernie was not so sure. He had been with his dad a couple of times when he had set a leg or sewn up cuts over at the Indian camp. He hadn't let on to his dad, but he had come away with a queasy stomach. He would rather be a reporter. He wrote articles for his high school paper all the time. Whatever he decided to be, he wouldn't get married for a long time. There were already too many women telling him what to do—his mother and four sisters.

Climbing to the opposite side of the ravine, he walked heavily across the meadow, trampling down the orange hawkweed. In five minutes he was climbing through the fence that confined the Bacons' cows to their pasture. Someone was plowing the back forty. He thought about going to see if it was Carl, but he was already late.

Mrs. Bacon held the screen door for him. She was one of those women who always said just what she was thinking, and she didn't mind if you said to her just what you thought, too.

She peered out at him. "Well, Ernie, you're a sight for sore eyes. You were nothing but a runt last year and look how you've taken off! I believe you're going to be as tall as Carl. Come on in, I'm just taking the bread out of the oven."

The kitchen was full of sunlight and delicious smells. He remembered all the good meals he had shared with the Bacon family around their big oak table, especially the breakfasts of eggs and pancakes, sausages and ham, fried potatoes, and two kinds of pie for dessert. Mrs. Bacon opened the oven of the wood stove. Inside were six golden brown loaves of bread. She took one out and cut off a large hunk. The soft warm bread buckled under the knife. She slathered it with pale home-churned butter and handed it to Ernie. "You want something to drink?"

"No thanks, I've got to be getting back. My mother needs the milk for the baby." The butter melted on the warm bread and ran down his chin.

"The baby! Don't tell me you've got a new baby at your house. Your ma's getting too old for that stuff. Here." She held out a second slice bigger than the first. "You finally get a boy this time?"

"Yes, his name's Leicester. Is that Carl out there plowing?"

"It better be. He's not going to have time to fool around with you this summer. We've had so much rain we might have to replant our corn. Anyhow, you'll have your hands full with the vegetable garden and your dad's orchard. You better get those fruit trees sprayed this week. You can come over and get our sprayer. You'll need some whitewash for the trunks, too. You camping out again?"

"Yes, ma'am."

"I never heard of such a thing. I'd think you'd be glad for a roof over your head. Next thing you know you'll turn into an Indian."

The basket she was filling with milk bottles and eggs was familiar. He had carried it back and forth between the farm and Windemere every summer since he could remember. She handed it to him. "Tell your ma the pullet'll be nice sized in a week or so. I don't suppose that makes *you* happy." It was well known that Ernie didn't much care for his job of killing and plucking the chickens and dressing them out. When Ernie grinned at her she nudged him in the ribs. "You're gettin' to be a real good-looking young man, Ernie. Those dimples won't do you any harm with the ladies, either."

When he got back to the cottage, Marce and his mother unpacked the basket. "Look at the cream on that milk," his mother said. "It's almost too thick to pour. You can't get milk that rich in the city. It might be a little *too* rich for the baby. We'll have to skim it. He's got a touch of colic."

"Don't I know it," Marce said. "I had to get up with him twice last night."

"I heard you, dear, and I appreciated it. If your father were here, he'd be doing the getting up. If I don't get my sleep at night, I get one of my headaches the next day. You'll be happy to know I've decided to get someone in to help out. After all, this is supposed to be our vacation."

"Who are you hiring?" Ernie asked. The year before they had had a German girl from Petoskey. His mother had discovered the girl had a fine singing voice and had made her practice her scales all day long while she made beds and washed dishes. Once they had a mother's helper who taught all the kids to say things in a foreign language, but when they had repeated the words to a man at the sawmill who spoke the same language, he had laughed until he doubled over and said he hadn't heard so many dirty words since his ma had kicked his pa out of the house.

"Mr. Lacour came by today to see if we had any odd jobs that needed doing while your dad was away. He said his daughter Nina was looking for work. I asked him to send her over tomorrow. I don't quite trust him, but she's a quiet, pretty little thing. I'm sure she'll do a good job."

Ernie was dumbfounded. Nina in his house. Every time he came over she'd be there. He'd never be able to get away from her. "What do you want to have an Indian in the house for?" he said. Marce and his mother both looked up, startled by the sharpness in his voice.

Sunny, who had walked into the kitchen in time to hear his remark, stared darkly at him. "Ernest Miller Hemingway, that's a stinking thing to say. Indians are just as good as you are anytime. They can catch fish by tickling their stomachs. That's more than you can do!"

"You can just send Sunny to get milk from the Bacons' after this," he shouted. "I've got plenty to do

with the fruit trees and the vegetables. I can't be spending all my time over here!" He slammed out of the cottage, leaving his mother and Marce staring at one another and Sunny with tears in her eyes. He knew he deserved her indignation for saying something so awful but
he'd never admit it.

He pulled hard on the oars, anxious to get back to the
solitude of his camp. He would keep away from Windemere. He wasn't going to let his sisters see how he felt
about Nina. Especially Sunny, who could always guess
what he was thinking. Anyhow, he was sick of being their
errand boy. Let them get along without him and see how
they liked it.

He was still angry as he climbed the hill to his tent.
He'd like to get his hands on the person who messed up
his campsite. As he walked toward his tent he saw what
looked like pieces of paper lazily turning over and over
in the breeze that blew up each afternoon at this time,
curling around the hills and shaking the tops of the trees.

He chased one of the sheets. As he got closer to it his
heart started pounding. It was a page from a book. Ernie
grabbed at it before it could flutter away again. A page
from his *African Game Trails*. Only it wasn't his. It belonged to the Oak Park Library and he'd have to pay for
it. It probably cost two or three dollars. He felt sick. It
wasn't just the money, but whoever it had been must have
known how he felt about books.

He ran toward the tent, scooping up the pages as he

went. There was only one thing worse the vandal could have done. He yanked the blankets off his cot. His shotgun was still there. Just before he left for the Bacon farm that morning, something made him hide it. At the time he had felt foolish but he was glad now he had followed his hunch.

His other books were all right but his duffel bag had been emptied and his clean clothes were scattered everywhere. It looked as though someone had deliberately ground them into the dirt with their boots. They had stepped on his pocket mirror and broken it, too.

The meanness made him feel sick. Why the senseless destruction? Only it wasn't senseless. It had a message. The message was clear. Someone was telling him to get out, that they didn't want him there.

Only minutes ago he had been thinking of this place as his. A place where no one could come without his permission. Now someone was saying *he* shouldn't be there.

No one was going to scare him away. He would find out who did it and get even. He would think of the worst thing he could do to them and he would do it. In the meantime he would set a trap.

4
Night Visitors

As soon as it was dark, Ernie grabbed his shotgun and climbed partway up one of the hemlocks, hiding himself among the thick green branches. Just let whoever it was come back. He was ready. But the longer he sat there, the more he knew he could never shoot someone, in spite of what they had done to his things. Still, he could give them a scare they wouldn't forget.

At first the novelty of being up in a tree in the middle of the night was fun. He passed the time trying to imagine how an owl or a raccoon might feel up there, waiting, just as he was, for its prey. Only animals had eyes that could see in the dark. Nothing was happening. He grew sleepy and afraid he might doze off and fall out of the tree. Finally, after it seemed he had been up there for hours, he climbed down sheepishly, glad no one had seen him. At least he didn't think anyone had. He told himself he could keep a watch from his tent window. A while later, looking out the window, he thought he saw something move at the treeline but it might have been a deer. Around midnight he fell asleep.

He was awakened in the night by someone or something brushing against his tent. He grabbed his gun. His hands were trembling so he could hardly hold it. He waited. For a long time everything was silent and then there it was again, a soft rubbing against the canvas. With his shotgun in one hand and a flashlight in the other, he forced himself to move stealthily out of the tent. Earlier in the evening he would have given a million dollars to have discovered someone there. Now he was praying hard that it had just been his imagination.

He switched on the flashlight, aiming it at the back of the tent where he had heard the noise. He saw a small black and white animal head for the woods. A skunk. He started to laugh and let out a whoop. With nothing but his shorts on he chased the skunk, shotgun in one hand, flashlight in the other. "Hey! Hey!" He was dancing through the woods yelling at the top of his voice, "Come on back here, you son of a bitch!" There was camaraderie in his voice. He loved that skunk. When the skunk escaped by disappearing into a hollow tree, he was pleased.

The next day was clear and bright. He worked hard whitewashing all the trunks of the fruit trees and pruning off the limbs that had suffered winter damage, wondering while he worked what Longfield looked like buried under three or four feet of snow. One winter he would find out. It didn't seem right to desert the land every fall. He wished his parents would move away from Oak Park and come up here to live. When he was on his own he would never live in a city. Cities were always telling you what to do.

After a hard day's work he returned hungry to his camp to find the skunk had fished his bacon out of the creek where he kept it cool in a waterproof tin. The lid was pried open and half the meat was missing. You could smell the skunk, too. He knew he couldn't have it around the camp. He'd have to get rid of it.

He dug a hole in the damp sandy soil near the spring for his food chest. By burying it he would keep his provisions cool and discourage the skunk. He had just lowered in the box when he caught sight of Sunny rowing across the lake. He stood up waiting for some sign that she had forgiven him for being such a darn fool about Nina's coming to work for them. He thought again how unsettling it was going to be to have Nina around all the time.

Sunny was waving her hand at him. He signaled back, relieved that she wasn't angry anymore. Maybe he'd let Sunny go after the skunk with him before it got dark.

"Ernie," Sunny was coming up from the beach holding a paper in her hand. "I brought you a ham sandwich and some apple pie and the Charlevoix *Courier.* "There's this neat serial in it all about an orphan girl named Zudora whose parent left her a twenty million dollar gold mine. That was where her dad got killed. And her uncle Ralph is her guardian, only he's pretending to be a mystic from India. He calls himself Hassam Ali. He wants to murder her and get her money but a young lawyer named John Storm is in love with her and he's going to try to save her." Sunny handed him the paper. "You want to read it?"

"I'll read it later," he said wolfing down the welcome food. "How come Mama let you take the boat out after supper?"

"I don't think she knows," Sunny said vaguely. "Anyhow, if I listened to her, I'd turn into a simp like Marce."

"Marce is OK."

"She wears shoes! Why are you dunking those hemlock branches in the spring, Ernie?"

"I'll show you." He flicked one of the branches at her and she dodged the wet spray. He had placed a flat boulder on the cover of his buried food chest so the skunk couldn't pry it off. Now he laid the wet branches on top of the boulder. "They'll keep the butter and meat cool," he explained.

"Why don't you just keep them in the spring like you did?"

"There's a skunk around here and he'd eat the stuff if I didn't have it covered up. They suck eggs right out of the shell. I'm going to shoot him. You want to help me track him down?"

"Sure, but why do you have to shoot him?"

"Because he ate my bacon and he might stink up the tent some night. Then I'd have to move everything and make a new camp and that's too much trouble." He got his gun and told her to keep behind him and be quiet. They headed for the edge of the woods. The June evenings seemed to stretch on forever. Yesterday had been the summer solstice—the longest day of the year. From now on the days would grow shorter. The thought saddened him.

Sunny wanted to ask him where they were going and what made a skunk smell and whether if they got too close to it they'd smell, too. But Ernie didn't appreciate a lot of chatter when he was hunting. As they moved silently along the edge of the woods she stopped to pick up a blue feather. Its ladder of black stripes told her it was from the bluejay's tail. A minute later she found some red wintergreen berries that made your mouth taste like chewing gum. She offered one to Ernie but he waved it away. She tried harder to concentrate on the hunting, but a part of her didn't want to find the skunk.

Ernie stopped and she watched while he lobbed a stone into a hollow stump.

There was a black and white flash and he raised his gun and fired. It happened so fast that it caught Sunny unprepared. She jumped at the sound of the explosion. He shot a second time and the skunk lay motionless.

"Dad would have had it on the first shot," he said. "It just moved too fast for me."

"Phew, it smells terrible. What are you going to do with it?"

"Have to bury it but not here."

Holding her nose she peered down at the skunk. Its fur was glossy black with a white stripe on its head and down either side of its back. Its hind paws were shaped like small human feet. She would never have admitted it to Ernie, but she didn't like hunting. Rather, she liked the hunting but she didn't like the killing part.

Ernie had cut a sapling. He attached the skunk to the end of the long pole and told her to get in the boat and hold it while he rowed. When they got a good distance from his camp he beached the boat and buried the skunk.

They rowed back toward the camp. The setting sun tinted the whole lake a pale liquid orange. The water dripping from the oars was orange. Even their hands and faces had an orange glow. Behind them the trees were black against the orange sky.

"You better get back before it's dark," Ernie said. "You can go fishing with me tomorrow."

"Ernie, will you teach me how to fish with artificial flies?"

"Sure."

She thought longingly of the tiny flies made of colored feathers and fur and horsehair Ernie and her dad made on winter evenings. With their plumy wings and bristling hackles they looked just like real flies. "Ernie," she said, "remember how I stood lookout for you last winter when you used Mom's music room for your boxing matches and brought you pails of water from the kitchen and cleaned up when you had that nosebleed?"

"Sure. That stage mother built in the music room made a great boxing ring."

"Ernie, would you teach me how to tie my own flies, too?"

"Sure I will. When you grow up you can tie your husband's flies."

"I'll tie my *own* trout flies," she said with emphasis. "I'm going to marry a man who knows how to cook like Dad does and I'm just going to fish all day." The prospect made her so happy she didn't even complain when Ernie hurried her home.

When he got back to his tent he found it was still warm inside from the sun beating down on the canvas all day. He kicked the blanket off his cot and settled down with the Charlevoix *Courier*. Shadows from his kerosene lantern decorated the walls of the tent with soft black shapes. A June bug sputtered against the window screen.

The *Courier* had a front page story about how the Charlevoix police were looking for a ring of deer poachers who were making a lot of money selling venison to restaurants down in Detroit. There was plenty of war news. The English and the Australians and the French were fighting the Turks on the peninsula of Gallipoli in the Dardanelles. He knew from his geography that this was the Hellespont that Byron had swum. He wanted to be like Byron. A writer and a warrior fighting for freedom.

He turned to an article about the new German submarines that could make the amazing speed of twelve knots under water and twenty-four above water. When they were submerged the submarines signaled to one another by ringing bells. A man sat in a soundproof room in one submarine and using a microphone he could pick up the vibrations moving through the water from the bell on the other submarine.

One of the subs had captured the Dutch ship *Batavia.* In the quiet of the northern Michigan night it seemed impossible that a big war was going on over in Europe. He thought of how the great ocean liner, the *Lusitania,* had been sunk less than two months ago. He began to invent a great story about submarines. Suppose America got into the war, although everyone said it wouldn't, but just suppose it did. He would join up right away and be an officer in a submarine and he and his men would glide silently across the bottom of the ocean hunting the Germans.

He would be Commander Hemingway. His opposite number in the German submarine would be Commander Schiller. He knew that was a real German name because their butcher in Oak Park was German and that was his name. The two submarines would meet in a fatal duel. He would destroy Commander Schiller's ship with his last torpedo. He wondered if the navy limited your ammunition like his dad did, to improve your aim. He didn't like the idea of killing Schiller. He could see him with his spiked helmet and blue eyes peering out of round steel eyeglasses just like the ones their butcher in Oak Park wore. That was the trouble with making up stories—you even got interested in the villains and didn't want to kill them off.

The two submarines were circling one another when a noise startled Ernie out of his daydream. It came from the direction of the spring. At first he thought it might be another skunk or a raccoon nosing around his food chest for something to eat, but a few seconds of careful listening told him the noises were human. Someone was moving around out there. He heard whoever it was lift the boulder from his foodbox and pry off the metal top. Ernie made his way toward the noise, his bare feet silent on the mossy ground. Just beneath his fear there was a feeling of excitement. You were never as alive as when you were afraid.

Whoever was there struck a match to look in the box. In the quick flare Ernie saw a figure bending over. It was Tommy Thrake. Ernie threw himself at Tommy, catching him off balance and toppling him over onto the ground.

Tommy slipped out of his hold and scrambled to his feet. "What'd you jump me for?" He brushed the sand off his clothes.

"What do you think you're doing going through my stuff?"

"Someone around here's shooting squirrels. I found where they'd been skinned. You've got a gun. I've seen you hunting."

"I haven't shot any squirrels."

"Then who did? You're around here all the time. You know who it is."

"If I did know, I wouldn't tell you. What's it to you anyhow?" Ernie would have to warn Ted Lacour.

"My dad's the game warden and I'm his deputy. He's gotta spend his time lookin' for those deer poachers so I'm supposed to keep an eye on the other stuff like squirrels."

"Well, you don't have any right to go into my private food chest." Ernie looked down at the ground. The remainder of his bacon and the butter he had carefully stowed away lay scattered in the dirt. He remembered the pages of his book blowing in the wind and how the stool he had made had been chopped into pieces. He felt a rage he had only known a few times before in his life. It grew in him until he thought if he didn't do something it would choke him. His camp was the place where he had thought he was safe from any prying. "You put all that stuff you messed up back in there just like you found it," he said in a voice hoarse with anger.

"Who's going to make me?" Tommy's voice had the overly defiant note of uncertain authority.

Ernie crouched down, right hip slightly forward, body bent, left arm stretched out, hands clenched into fists. He waited for Tommy to take a boxing stance. He was pretty sure he could outbox him.

But in the next second Tommy was rushing at him and only Ernie's quick dodge saved him from a kick in the groin. There wasn't going to be any boxing match. He saw Tommy reach for a stone and tackled him. They were both about the same size. Ernie was mad enough to fight someone twice as big, but Tommy had gone all limp and pliable. It was like wrestling with an old pillow. Angry as Ernie was, he couldn't bring himself to hit someone that spineless.

"Let me go!" Tommy shouted. "You let me go or I'll tell my father."

Disgusted, Ernie stood up. "Why don't you tell your father how you tore up my book and threw my clothes all around?"

Tommy's mouth dropped open. "I never did. Why would I do that?"

"You're lying. You're too mealy-mouthed to admit it." But strangely, Ernie believed him. Tommy was a toad and a sneak, but he looked too scared to have tried anything like that and too dumb to cover it up if he had. The fight went out of Ernie.

Tommy saw that Ernie wouldn't come after him and bolted for the woods. When he was at a safe distance he called out, "We'll get 'cha. You'd just better be careful what you do."

Ernie gathered up his food. He shouldn't have let Tommy get off so easily. He was sure Tommy would find a way to get back at him. He told himself he wouldn't do anything dumb that would get him into trouble. But he knew himself too well to believe it.

5
Barn Dance

To reach the town of Horton Bay they rowed from Windemere across to Longfield Farm. From there it was a three-mile hike over green hills. At the top of each hill they caught a glimpse of the vivid blue of Pine Lake stretched out below them. As they dropped down the hill, the lake disappeared. The green hills and blue lake seemed to go on forever, as though they were unrolling from endless sheets of colored paper.

Sunny was carrying an overnight bag Marce had lent her. It had a lock with its own key. She wore the key on a chain around her neck so she wouldn't lose it, enjoying the bounce of the cool metal against her chest as she walked along. Ernie had a canvas duffel bag slung over his shoulder. There was going to be a barn dance that night in Horton Bay and Sunny had talked Ernie into taking her. Then Ernie had talked his mother into letting Sunny go. He probably couldn't have if his father had been there. His father thought dancing was sort of evil but his mother believed dancing was healthy for you. She had even talked his father into letting them take dancing lessons.

Ernie was glad he had the trip to look forward to. Camping in the woods away from people was fine when everything was going all right. But when something was bothering you, you had too much time to think about it. Right now he was trying to forget about his fight the night before with Tommy Thrake.

There wasn't much to Horton Bay: a sprinkling of neat frame houses under big elm trees, a township school, a Methodist church, Fox's General Store, and Jim Dilworth's blacksmith shop painted barn red. In the quiet summer afternoon the small country village looked as though nothing had ever happened there, but Ernie knew that twenty years before, Horton Bay had been a booming lumber port with a sawmill that turned out thousands of board feet of white pine. Big schooners had sailed from Lake Michigan into Pine Lake and up to the dock beside the mill. The mill was gone now and only the long dock remained, stretching out into the lake as though it believed a great billowing sail might appear on the horizon at any moment.

Ernie and Sunny were headed for the Dilworths' house, Pinehurst, where they would be staying. Although they weren't really any relation, the families were good friends and they had always called the Dilworths Aunty Beth and Uncle Jim. Aunty Beth served chicken and trout dinners to people. It wasn't exactly a restaurant. It was just that her reputation for chicken and homemade pies had brought hungry strangers to her door. She had started feeding them and making money doing it.

At the sight of the blacksmith shop, Sunny said, "Let's go see Uncle Jim before we go to Pinehurst. Aunty Beth's food is awfully good, but Uncle Jim's blacksmith shop is one of the best places in the world."

When they got to the smithy they found Jim Dilworth shoeing a horse for Simon Green. The fire in the forge was an angry red. "Well, you two," Jim Dilworth greeted them. "I hear you're going to spend the night with us. Come for the barn dance did you? I suppose you got a string of beaux going to give you a big rush at the dance, Sunny."

"I don't even know how to dance," Sunny said, "and even if I did, I'm not sure I would. It looks dumb. Hello, Mr. Green."

Simon Green was a rich Indian who farmed a large, prosperous acreage. His mahogany brown face was carved into creases like some old ornate piece of furniture. His eyes were black and sharp as a jay's. He enjoyed being rich and spent a lot of time at Fox's General Store urging Mr. Fox to improve the quality of his merchandise. "I don't know why you sell such cheap tobacco," he'd complain. "My father could get better stuff than this by trading nothing more than the skin of a skunk." Simon Green had a taste for candy and when he wasn't smoking his pipe he'd be sitting in a chair on the front porch of the store, working his way down a long strap of licorice.

Simon clapped Ernie on the shoulder. "I hear you're nearly as good a shot as your dad. He ever tell you about the time we were shooting partridge together? Flushed them out right next to Horton Creek and before I even got my gun up your dad had dropped three of them. That's real shooting," he said appreciatively.

Ernie ran a hand along the flank of Mr. Green's horse. He felt proud when someone praised his father's marksmanship, but he felt a little jealous, too. When he drew his hand away from the horse it was wet with the horse's sweat.

The horse was standing quietly while Jim Dilworth hammered nails through the horseshoe. After each nail was tapped in, the smith bent the nail over to secure it. When he finished the shoeing he took one of the iron nails and welded it into a ring on his anvil. He plunged the ring into cold water. The hot metal hissed and sizzled. Handing it to Sunny he said, "You just remember, young lady, I'm the first man ever gave you a ring."

Delighted, Sunny slipped it onto her finger. Its weight made her hand heavy. "Why doesn't it hurt the horse to have horseshoes pounded into its feet?" she asked.

"They don't pound them into the horse's feet," Ernie explained, "just into its hooves. That's like your fingernails. It doesn't hurt to cut your fingernails does it?"

"Your brother's right." Jim Dilworth took out a red

print handkerchief as big as a small tablecloth and rubbed the sweat from his face. He folded it back up into a small neat square and put it into his pocket. "Why don't you two get out of this hot place and go up and see Aunty Beth? She's been bakin' up a storm for you. I'll catch up with you at supper."

After they left, Simon Green said, "That boy's near as good a hunter as his dad whether he thinks so or not. But he'll shoot at anything. That'll get him in trouble one of these days."

"Maybe he'll be lucky and grow up first," Dilworth replied.

After Ernie and Sunny had left their bags at Pinehurst and collected a handful of molasses cookies still warm from the oven, they walked down the road that led from the village to Pine Lake. Long before they came to the big lake they could smell its fish smell and see the wheeling gulls. The bay was sheltered by a long point. The beach that curved around to the point was crescent shaped with a wide sandy strip separating the lake from the fringe of alder and willow that grew along the shore. Beyond the shrubs were the cedar and tamarack that marked the swampy area around a little brook. Ernie had camped out overnight near there when he had come to fish for bass in the lake. He remembered the slap of the waves against the stony beach and how the smell of cedar drifted over each morning from the brook.

Pine Lake was a lot bigger than Walloon and because

it emptied into Lake Michigan it had a different feeling. "From right where we're standing," Ernie told Sunny, "we could take a boat and go north to Mackinac Island and around to Lake Huron and Lake Ontario and down the St. Lawrence right to the Atlantic Ocean. From the ocean we could go to England or Spain or past the Rock of Gibraltar and all the way down to Africa."

"Why don't we do that, Ernie? We've got a boat. Only we'd have to be back in time for school in the fall."

"You could learn a lot more traveling around Europe than you could at school."

"You couldn't learn arithmetic or how to parse a sentence," Sunny said. "Anyhow it says in the *Courier* there's a war in Europe. If we went over there we'd have to fight in the war, wouldn't we?"

"Sure. I wouldn't mind being a soldier."

"Could I be one?"

"No, you'd have to be a nurse or a spy."

"I wouldn't mind being a nurse but spies have to live on bread and water." The thought of bread and water made Sunny hungry. She was remembering the two chocolate pies she had seen cooling on a windowsill at Pinehurst.

For their dinner at Pinehurst there were bowls of chicken soup with homemade noodles and little gold beads of melted chicken fat floating on the top. There was fried chicken with your choice of dark or light meat and mashed potatoes swimming in milk gravy and fresh peas from the Dilworth garden and bread and butter pickles and hot biscuits with wild strawberry jam and brandied peaches, which Aunty Beth didn't serve to everyone because so many people in Horton Bay were temperance. For dessert there was the chocolate pie with a thick layer of whipped cream on top.

Aunty Beth shook her head as she cut Ernie a second piece of pie. "I don't know why this chocolate pie doesn't hold up when you cut it. It looks sloppy on the plate. Sunny, will you have another piece?"

"Yes, ma'am."

"I'm glad to see you have an appetite. I can't stand girls sitting around with nothing better to think about than their waistlines. It isn't healthy."

"I hear the dance is going to be a big affair," Uncle Jim said. "People'll be coming from the farms all around here and from Charlevoix, too." He was spooning the whipped cream off the top of his pie, being careful not to cut into the chocolate. He liked to save the cream for last.

Aunty Beth said, "If there's going to be a lot of strangers there, Ernie, I don't know if you ought to take Sunny. She's a little on the young side."

"Aunty *Beth,*" Sunny pleaded.

"Ernie'll keep an eye on her," Uncle Jim reassured his wife.

"Well, you get her back early. And give your feet a good washing, Sunny. I hope you brought shoes?"

"Yes, ma'am, and my good dress."

Uncle Jim smiled. "While you're washing, you'd

better wash away some of that chocolate pie from around your mouth."

The dance was held in a big barn just outside of town. On one side of the barn, horse-drawn carriages and wagons were tied to posts. The automobiles were on the other side where their backfires and sputterings wouldn't bother the horses. There were Fords and Packards and Hudsons, Maxwells and Wintons and Chevrolets. Ernie stopped to run his hand over the long sleek body of a Packard touring car. It was a rich maroon color with shiny brass headlamps. "I wouldn't mind having that baby," Ernie said.

"Why doesn't Dad get a car?"

"Costs too much. A car like that must be worth plenty."

Sunny wished she could buy Ernie a car. She thought of the allowance of eleven cents a week she got for shaking the sand out of the rugs each morning and sighed.

The music drifted out to them on the summer night like someone sending a pleasant message. They hurried into the lighted barn, pushing their way past some people who were coming outside to cool off. The barn looked festive. Red and yellow paper lanterns hung from the rafters and crepe paper streamers crisscrossed the room. The orchestra was playing "By the Light of the Silvery Moon" and the dancers were singing along. Sunny clutched at Ernie's hand to keep from being swept away in the crowd but Ernie wasn't paying any attention to her. He was busy trying to signal Bill Smith, a friend of his who spent his summers at Horton Bay. Bill was standing on the other side of the barn. Ernie turned to Sunny. "I'm going over to see Bill. You stay here and don't get into any trouble."

Feeling abandoned, Sunny sat down on a chair and looked around. The barn floor had been swept clear of straw and sprinkled with wax to make the floor slippery. Except for a faint odor of cow and a few startled mice running in and out of the wheat bins, it wasn't like a barn at all.

Everyone seemed to know everyone else. Sunny felt awkward sitting by herself. The high-ceilinged barn still retained the afternoon heat. She would have liked a glass of cold lemonade but she was afraid if she walked across the room to the refreshment table, Ernie would say she was tagging after him. She looked around for someone familiar. The Dilworths' son, Wesley, was there with his new wife, Katherine, but they were dancing with spoony looks on their faces and didn't see her. Her shoes, which she hadn't worn since Oak Park, had grown too small and hurt her feet. The collar of her starched organdy dress rubbed against the back of her neck and her puffed sleeves prickled whenever she moved. She began to wish she hadn't come.

Across the room Ernie was trying not to show how impressed he was with Bill Smith, who was already in college and who looked plenty sophisticated in a striped flannel jacket.

"How come I haven't seen you all summer?" Bill asked him.

"My dad's not coming up until next month so I've got to keep an eye on my mom and the girls. I've been doing a lot of fishing, too." Ernie added. He was a better fisherman than Bill.

A couple of girls Ernie didn't recognize were standing at the other end of the table stealing glances at the two boys and giggling. "Maybe we should ask them to dance," he said. One of the girls had curly blond hair and a blue dress that was a lot shorter than the dresses of the other girls. It was the shortest dress Ernie had ever seen on a girl.

Bill shrugged. "No hurry. The girls'll wait for us."

"Sure," Ernie said, embarrassed at appearing too eager. "How's college?" he asked changing the subject.

"It's fine, but I don't know if I'll get a chance to finish."

"What do you mean?"

"I was in Charlevoix yesterday and I heard the Coast Guard is being issued Krag rifles."

"Rifles?"

"That's not all." Bill lowered his voice. The music had stopped and the dancers were crowding around the table helping themselves to lemonade punch and pieces of applesauce cake. He motioned Ernie over to an empty corner of the barn.

Ernie took a quick look across the room at Sunny. She was sitting on a chair. He saw that she had worked her shoes nearly off and had them balancing on her toes. He guessed she was all right.

"The Coast Guard is digging trenches along the Lake Michigan beaches," Bill told him.

"Do they think the Germans are going to come over here and capture Charlevoix?" Ernie said. "They got all they can do to get hold of France."

"I'm just telling you what I saw," Bill said. "But if America gets in the war I might sign up."

"Listen, Bill." Ernie was excited. "Why don't we take off for Canada? I've been thinking about joining the Canadian army." He hadn't until Bill talked about signing up. Now it seemed like a great idea. He imagined Nina seeing him off, tears in her eyes. And he wouldn't have to take care of a bunch of women.

"I think you have to be eighteen. How old are you, Ernie?"

"I'm going to be seventeen." He didn't add that his birthday was nearly a year away. "Anyhow, I could pass for eighteen and I'm a darn good shot. That's what they want, isn't it?"

Now it was Bill who changed the subject. "Hey," he said, "that slick number with the blue dress and the silver shoes is all alone. I'd sure like to get my arms around her. Let's go over and see which one of us she picks."

Sunny watched Ernie and Bill move through the crowded floor toward a girl in a blue dress. The girl's hair was crimped into a hundred little ringlets. Sunny had watched Marce and Ursula crimping their hair with a curling iron. You could smell burning hair all over the house. The girl was making a big show of laughing at what Ernie and Bill were saying to her but before Sunny could see what happened, a boy came up to her.

"Hello, my name's Alfred Wingstead. You care to dance?" Although it was near the end of July, his face was a pale white like the underbelly of a fish. He had watery blue eyes and red hair brushed into a big wave that shelved out over his forehead.

Sunny was going to tell him she didn't know how to dance but across the room she could see Ernie was dancing with the girl in the blue dress. She thought she would like to have her brother see her sailing across the dance floor with a boy. Reaching down she stuck a finger in the heel of each shoe and squeezed her feet painfully back into them. As she stood up she felt a little foolish. Where did your hands go when you danced? She stole a look at the other dancers and tried to copy them. It felt funny being so close to a boy. His shirt had a nice freshly ironed smell, but his hair stunk like rotten peaches. She guessed he had plastered something on it to make the shelf.

"Don't push," he complained. "You're supposed to follow me."

"How do I know where you're going?"

"I push *you*."

"Why should you push me if I can't push you?"

"I'm fifteen," he said. "How old are you?"

"I'm fourteen," she lied. Maybe he would believe her. She was tall for her age.

"Then how come you never danced before?"

"In the city we do different dances," she said haughtily.

"What city do you come from?"

"Oak Park."

"That's practically in the country," he said. "We live right in Chicago. On Ontario Street."

Alfred's hand was moist and sticky. She longed to pull her own hand away and wipe it off. He had adenoids or something. Each time he breathed he wheezed hot little breezes into her ear. She looked around for Ernie and the girl with the blue dress but they were on the other side of the barn.

"I think you should bend your knees a little. You're too stiff," Alfred told her.

"I'm not," she said, stopping suddenly. "And my feet hurt from you stepping all over them."

"You want to go outside?" he asked her.

"Sure," she said with relief.

He held on to her arm, guiding her toward the door. "Let go." She shook off his arm. "I can walk by myself."

Outside they passed a couple on their way back into the barn. The couple was holding hands. With her free hand the girl was smoothing her hair. The boy was wiping something off his face with his handkerchief.

"I guess they must have had a pretty good time," Alfred snickered. But Sunny wasn't paying attention. After the hot, stuffy barn she was taking deep gulps of cool night air.

"You wanna go and sit in our automobile? We've got a new Packard touring car."

"Sure." Sunny was thrilled. She couldn't wait to tell Ernie she had actually sat in the car he had been admiring. He'd be plenty sorry he hadn't stayed with her instead of chasing some ninny wearing a dress so short you could see her knobby knees.

They passed other couples sitting in cars. That must be what you did when you got tired of dancing, she decided. When they got to the Packard, Sunny started to climb in the front seat, hoping Alfred would let her sit behind the steering wheel where she could pretend to drive, but instead he told her to get into the back. She was disappointed but she did what he said. After all, it was his car and she was relieved just to be sitting down. In a minute she had her shoes off. The leather seat felt cool on her back and legs.

Alfred was inching closer to her. "You're crowding me," she complained.

Instead of moving away he put an arm around her neck. The wheezing when he breathed was louder than ever. She pushed him away.

"What'd you do that for?" he asked.

"I don't like you breathing all over me."

"Then why'd you come out here?"

Before she could answer him the car door was yanked open. "What do you think you're doing with my sister?" Ernie had Alfred by the lapel of his jacket and was dragging him from the car. Alfred shrunk into his suit like a turtle into his shell. Ernie stood over him glowering.

Sunny found herself feeling sorry for Alfred. Why was Ernie so angry with him? "It was too hot in the barn, Ernie," she explained, "so we just came out here to cool off." She climbed down beside Alfred.

Ernie was yelling at Alfred, giving him a shake with every word. "You don't have any right to sit in a car with my sister. She's only eleven years old,"

Sunny was mortified at having her age shouted out like that. "*Ernie*, let him go," she said indignantly. "I don't know why you're so angry. I *wanted* to come outside. My feet hurt."

Ernie released Alfred's jacket. In a second he was streaking off into the darkness. "Where are your shoes?" Ernie was staring at Sunny's stockinged feet.

"I forgot. They're in the car."

"You had no business getting undressed in the car."

"I didn't get *undressed*. I took off my shoes. What's the matter with that? I go barefoot all the time." She thought Ernie had taken leave of his senses.

"You come on back to the barn with me and this time you stay put."

"How come you're so mad, Ernie?"

"Girls don't get into cars with boys unless they want to get necked!"

Necking! With Alfred! Sunny was horrified. She would have died first. She tailed silently along behind Ernie. All the fun had gone out of the dance. "That girl with the blue dress you were dancing with," she said.

"What about her?" Ernie snapped.

Sunny gave him a smug look. "She and Bill Smith were sitting in the car we just passed."

6
How To Be a Lady

Ernie's days began to fall into an easy pattern. He worked in the vegetable garden early in the morning before the July sun turned everything into glittering white heat. Afternoons he and Sunny went fishing. Sunny had progressed from baiting her own hook to baiting Ernie's as well. She was willing to row for him so he could troll for lake trout and bass. In return he taught her the fine points of trout fishing like rubbing the sections of your fishing pole along the side of your nose to grease them so the sections would slide together and how to wax your line and leave the leader unwaxed so the line would float on the water and the leader would sink, leaving the fly at the end of it looking like it was skimming along the water. He had shown her how to cast the fly on a riffle or a whirlpool and how to work it in close to the shore where the lazy trout were hiding in the shade of the river bank.

Before he sent the fish back to Windemere with his sister, he cleaned them and together the two of them buried the entrails around the fruit trees. His dad had taught him how to do that. "That's what the Indians used to use for fertilizer," his father had told him.

Sunny carried messages back and forth from Ernie's camp to the cottage. Nina was working at Windemere now and he was keeping his distance. There were days, though, when his mother wanted him and then a signal would be hoisted from the flagpole on the dock—usually a white dish towel or a diaper—and he would have to row over.

A dish towel was flying from the dock that morning, but he took his time about answering the summons. He was watching two loons swimming on the lake. One of them was probably the one he had heard his first night. The other loon was its mate.

"Crazy as a loon," people said, and that was true. The two loons had turned over on their backs. Their feet were stuck straight up in the air. They slapped their wings against the water, sending up plumes of spray. Then they tipped right side up and swam at one another, splashing like two children. The loon was a handsome bird, larger than a duck, with dots and bars of black and white and a black velvety head with a long pointed patent leather beak and wild yellow eyes.

Dr. Hemingway knew how to stuff birds. Ernie wondered if his dad would like a loon to stuff. Only they were having so much fun. Besides, if he were caught shooting one he could be arrested. Twice now he had seen Tommy Thrake skulking around near his camp, just waiting to get him on something.

Ernie heard Marce's voice hallooing to him across the lake. He returned her call. Startled by the noise, the loons shrieked their own halloos and flew off to find a more solitary spot. Ernie thought they were lucky not to have a lot of sister loons screeching for them.

When Ernie got to the cottage he found a general air of busyness. Marce was on her knees, a row of bristling pins in her mouth, working on Ursula's party dress. Sunny was curled up in one of the window seats so absorbed in the newspaper that she didn't even look up when Ernie came in. His mother had Carol pinioned between her knees, snipping at her hair. "Well, Ernie," she smiled up at him, "you've gotten to be a stranger. Carol, stand still so I can get these bangs even. With all that hair hanging over your forehead, no one's been able to see your face for a month. I'm not even sure we'll recognize you."

"How come all the fuss?" Ernie asked.

"We're going to the opera in Charlevoix tomorrow night," Ursula said. "It's going to be 'Cavalleria Rustycanna.' "

"*Rusticana*, dear. Pronounced 'roosticana,' " their mother corrected Ursula.

"Roostercana. And *Anthony and Cleopatra*. Read what it says about the operas in the *Courier*, Sunny."

"Hold your horses," Sunny answered. "I'm just finishing the serial. Wu Chang is trying to get Zudora to elope with him by hypnotizing her and he and Ali Hassam are going to spirit her out of the country, only John Storm learns about their plot, and . . ."

"Sunny, dear, I can't think that lurid trash is suitable reading matter for a young girl. Please stop your squirming, Carol." Mrs. Hemingway was dusting bits of hair from Carol's face with a lace handkerchief.

"The hair gets into my nose when you do that and makes me sneeze."

"You want to hear about the opera, Ernie?" Sunny opened the paper to a large half-page ad. "Costumes of Egypt," she read. "Downfall of the Roman Empire. Death of Cleopatra. Quaint Sicilian village."

"Tell him what the singers' names are," Marce said, giggling.

"Mirth Carmen, Mercedes Dalmada, Basil Horsefall . . ."

"Basil *Horsefall!* I don't believe it." Ernie grabbed the paper. The girls were laughing. "That *is* his name. Listen to this." He read in a high falsetto, "In an interview the *prima donna* Mirth Carmen said, 'As a child it was dinned into me to save my voice but I've never been able to hold back. I throw my whole body and soul into it. I know that I'll burn out young but I'd rather be a spendthrift than a miser.' "

"That's nonsense," his mother said. "Ernie, why don't you come with us tomorrow night?"

"And see Basil Horsefall fall on his bass! No thanks!" The girls snickered.

Ernest Hemingway carrying his fly rod case along railroad tracks in northern Michigan.

Ernie on the shore of Walloon Lake.

"Windemere," the Hemingway family's summer cottage.

The living room at Windemere.

Ernie the game bird hunter in his preteen years.

Photo: John F. Kennedy Library

Hemingway in his element: landing a trout on a northern Michigan stream.

On a hiking trip.

The Hemingway family home in Oak Park, Illinois.

Family portrait taken in Ernie's early adult years: from left, Dr. Hemingway, Leicester, Sunny, Ursuline, Ernest, Mrs. Hemingway, Carol, and Marcelline.

The pathless woods.

"Ernie! That's not a nice thing to say. Your father would be very unhappy to hear that kind of talk. Which reminds me, he sent you a letter. I'm finished with you, Carol. Go and get Ernie's letter."

Reading his father's letter over to himself, Ernie could hear Dr. Hemingway's gentle voice. Even after all these years it was a surprise hearing that mild voice emerge from his father's strong face with its black beard and intense black eyes.

600 North Kenilworth   *August 7, 1915*

Dear Ernie,

Your mother has written me about the fine job you are doing taking care of the garden and orchard at Longfield. I knew that I could depend on you. However, she also mentions that you are keeping to yourself a good deal of the time and consequently, they don't see much of you at Windemere. I know the pleasures of camping out, having done a good deal of it myself when I was your age. However, you must remember that while your mother and the girls are alone, I depend upon you to take my place and be there whenever needed.

I want you to know what a fine young man I believe you are growing into. When I get up there we will have some long walks in the woods together and some good fishing.

Affectionately yours,
Your father

Reading the letter Ernie discovered that he missed his father. He was sixteen. At that age you were supposed to be independent of your parents. Hadn't he proved his independence by living in the tent for the past two summers? Still there were things he could learn from his father. His father knew a lot about nature. When you walked through the woods with him, he'd see a bird long before you did. He'd give you the Latin name for it and he was right. Ernie had checked him in his copy of *Birds of Nature*.

His mother was always after Ernie to practice his cello. She took all of them to concerts and operas and museums. She was sure all her children were going to be famous artists and musicians. Sometimes he got sick of that stuff. It was all right if you *felt* like doing it, but a lot of the time you didn't. His dad understood that.

Sunny gave a deep sigh, breaking in on his thoughts. "It's going to be three more days before the next installment and Zudora is fleeing through a storm with Ali Hassam right behind her, a scimitar, whatever that is, in his hand. You ought to write serials, Ernie. That story you wrote for the school magazine was nearly as good as this one. Then you could slip me the installments so I wouldn't have to wait to find out what happens." She threw down the newspaper. "Why don't we go fishing, Ernie?"

"Will you take me, too? I haven't been out with you once this year," Ursula complained.

Neither have I," Carol said.

"You can all come," Ernie told them. He was thinking of how his father had said to keep an eye on his sisters.

"No, thanks, not me," Marce announced. "I want to finish sewing my dress for tomorrow night."

"You got someone from the Chicago Club or the Belvedere you want to impress?" Ernie teased her. The wealthy resorters who belonged to those Charlevoix clubs had plushy summer homes and a lot of servants. Dr. Hemingway was skeptical of that kind of vacation. He thought you might as well stay in the city.

"As a matter of fact," his mother announced, "this time *I'm* going fishing with Ernie and the rest of you can stay home."

Ernie winced. Taking his mother out fishing was a nuisance. In the first place she weighed a hundred and eighty pounds. She wasn't fat, just big and solid. To be an opera singer, she said you had to have "a little heft" behind your voice. In Oak Park she was choir director at the Third Congregational Church. Standing there in her choir robes, waving her hands around, she looked plenty impressive, and if the hymn were one of her favorites like "A Mighty Fortress," or "Amazing Grace," her deep rich voice filled the church. She composed music, too. Sometimes you'd wake up in the middle of the night and hear her trying out some new arrangement on the piano.

The other thing was when she went fishing she took a lot of junk with her. A great big cartwheel of a hat because she sunburned easily, a smelly mosquito repellent made out of citronella and castor oil, a big jug of ice water, a pillow to sit on, and a book to read in case the fish weren't biting. The worst thing, though, was that sometimes she'd just start singing in the boat at the top of her lungs because she said your voice sounded so good over the water. Ernie was afraid everyone around the lake would think she was nuts.

The girls were sent to round up his mother's hat and pillow. "Nina," Mrs. Hemingway called into the kitchen, "will you come here for a minute, dear?" Nina came out of the kitchen with the baby in her arms. She was wearing a white cotton pinafore and her long black hair was tied back with one of Ursula's ribbons. With her hair skinned back like that, she looked older to Ernie. They smiled politely at one another.

"Nina, will you fix me a jug of ice water? Ernie, you go and chip some ice for her."

Ernie trailed along behind Nina. When they got into the kitchen he asked, "How do you like working here?" It was a dumb question. What did he expect her to say— that she hated it and they were all bums?

"I like it a lot." Nina sounded as though she meant it. "Your mother's good to me. And I like taking care of babies." She put Leicester down in his jumper, gently untangling his fingers from her hair. "Dad brought home a fawn once that was just a few months old. It was pretty but it kicked you if you tried to hold it in your arms."

"What happened to it?"

"After it grew a little my dad was going to butcher it

but Ted and I let it go. My dad had trained it to come when he whistled, though, so he went out in the woods and whistled and got it back. I guess we needed the meat."

Ernie sneaked a look at Nina's face to see if telling the story had bothered her. If it did, she wasn't letting on. He opened the icebox and jabbed at the big block of ice with a pick. Nina held out the jug and he dropped the chips into it.

"Ted says to tell you it won't be long before the caddis hatch is on and you can get plenty of trout."

"Will you come with us?" Ernie asked, forgetting his resolve to stay away from Nina.

"Ted'll think I'm in the way."

"You tell Ted I said it's all right if you want to come."

"Ernie," his mother called, "I'm ready."

The girls stood on the dock laughing and waving as though he and his mother were off on a cruise around the world. He wished he could throw all four of them in the lake. They knew how he felt about fishing expeditions with his mother.

"Have a wonderful time," they yelled at the top of their voices.

He glowered at them, but they only waved harder. A hundred feet or so from the shore was a weedbed where they usually fished for perch. He put up the oars and reached for the anchor.

"No, Ernie, I feel lucky today. Let's try for some pike."

Ernie sighed and headed for the deeper water. "Trying for pike" would take most of the afternoon but it was hard not to catch his mother's enthusiasm. Under the big hat her face was expectant and cheerful, like a child on the way to a party. She had managed to get her shoes and stockings off without showing more than an inch of leg under her long skirt and was wriggling her pink toes, which were surprisingly slim and graceful.

While his mother fished one side of the boat, Ernie fished the other. Although she didn't fish often, she was competitive, taking her fishing seriously, determined to catch a fish. He was careful to bait her line with the biggest minnows, ones that would appeal to a pike who needed a generous mouthful for all those rows of sharp teeth.

"Ernie, dear, you don't mind if I have a little talk with you?"

His heart sank. The fishing had probably been a ruse to get him away from the girls and give him a lecture. Had he done something wrong? He couldn't think of anything recent, but there were enough things in the past to make him feel guilty and keep a wary silence.

"It's about Sunny, Ernie. I'm afraid she's spending too much time with you."

He was startled. "What's the matter with that?"

"Well, she's almost twelve. Little girls become young ladies at that age." Marce had been kept out of school during her twelfth year and so had Ursula. His parents had explained it was a "difficult" year for young girls and they needed extra care. They hadn't kept *him* out of school when he was twelve and as far as he could tell, keeping Marce and Ursula home had only made them restless and resentful at having to miss school and end up behind their classmates. What's more, it had meant that Marce and he ended up in the same class, which he hated. "Sunny *likes* to spend time with me," he protested.

"That may be, dear, but I wonder if *you* don't enjoy—just a little bit, mind you—having someone around who looks up to you so much. I'm sure that's very satisfying, but it gives you a somewhat exaggerated idea of your importance. Sunny has real musical talent, Ernie. She plays the piano better than anyone else in the family. I don't want her to get in the habit of running around outdoors all the time or she'll never get back to her practicing. You can't be a serious musical artist and a tomboy at the same time."

Ernie wasn't sure about the first part of his mother's reprimand, but the last part was unfair. "What's the matter with being a tomboy? Dad taught all the girls how to shoot, didn't he? And they've all used his .22. He's even let them help him mold the bullets for Big Ed." Big Ed was Dr. Hemingway's most serious gun. He had carried it on his hunting trips to the Smoky Mountains before he was married. No one was allowed to touch it.

"I sometimes think your father forgets his daughters are growing into young ladies. It's important that Sunny learn some feminine graces and stop acting like a . . . EEEOOW!!!" His mother began screaming at the top of her voice and yanking back on her fishing pole. Ernie looked quickly around to see if there were any boats nearby. Mercifully there weren't. His mother's loud musical screams were like something out of a German opera, where they had those big lady warriors riding around on horses shouting at one another. He had seen an opera like that in Chicago and he and his sisters had to keep punching one another hard so they wouldn't laugh out loud. Probably his mother's yelling could pierce right through the cottages around the lake and back to the Bacons' farm.

"Ernie! Ooh! I've *got* one! He must be enormous!" She tried to hang on to the arcing pole.

"Give him some line, Momma. Don't jerk like that. You'll lose him. Calm down." Her hat had slipped over to one side of her head and her hair, always so neat, had come unfastened. She stamped her bare feet in excitement.

"It's a big one. I *know* it!" She was hanging so far over the edge of the boat that Ernie had to heel out on the opposite side to keep them from overturning. "I've got you!" she shouted into the water. Either the fish had been stunned by her screams or it was beginning to tire. The line had stopped stripping off the spool.

"Set the reel and don't let him get any slack," Ernie said. He was caught up in the contest with the fish now and wasn't thinking about being embarrassed. He maneuvered the boat so the fish couldn't swim under it and break the tension on the line.

His mother began reeling in. "Look at the size of that pike, Ernie! It must be three feet long if it's an inch."

He got out the landing net and slipped it under the fish. Pikes were ugly, long and snaky looking. Almost prehistoric. This was a big one, seven or eight pounds, easy.

"Let *me* do it, Ernie." She grabbed the net out of his hand.

"You'll get your dress all wet and fishy."

"I don't care." She heaved at the net and emptied the fish onto the bottom of the boat where it thrashed around. Wielding the heavy thermos bottle like a hammer, she gave the pike a series of lethal blows. It twitched once or twice and obligingly expired. His mother's hat had fallen off altogether and her dress was splattered with water and blood from the pike's struggle, but her expression was jubilant.

Ernie thought all she lacked was a suit of armor and a spear held high over her head. He was laughing so hard he could hardly get his words out. "What was it you were telling me about how important it was for Sunny to learn feminine graces?" he asked. "I'll bet that pike didn't think you were a lady!"

The girls refused to let him go until they heard how the fish had been caught. "I wish you could have seen the delicate way Momma beat the fish to death," he told them, giving his mother a meaningful wink. Marce took a picture of his mother holding up the vanquished pike. The pike's mouth was drawn up in a sleepy smile. The smile on his mother's face was radiant. Ernie stayed on to help consume the fish. Carried in by the girls with great ceremony, it was swimming again, but this time in a delicious egg and lemon sauce.

After dinner he sat in the kitchen finishing off a second piece of strawberry shortcake and watching Ursula and Nina, big white aprons tied around their waists, do the dishes. The kitchen windows had been opened to let out some of the heat from the wood stove. Looking out he could almost feel the darkness as it crept out of the beechwood forest and onto the green lawn. A whippoorwill was calling, at first from a distance, and then almost directly over their heads. It appeared each night just as the last light was leaving the sky. Nina held her dishcloth in midair, listening to the receding call while a trickle of soap suds ran down her arm. "My grandfather used to say you should never let a whippoorwill fly over you. He dreamed once that the whippoorwill carries the night with him like a dark shadow and whatever it passes over will disappear."

"Why would he believe a dream?" Ursula asked.

"Dreams are important to Indians. My grandfather wouldn't name my mother until he had the right dream. When it came he dreamed he was climbing up a hill. At the top of the hill he looked down and saw a lake. So her Indian name is 'Lake from the Top of the Hill.'"

"That's the prettiest name I've ever heard," Ursula said. She had a dreamy look on her face.

"My grandfather thought if you dreamed something important, you had to do it. There was a young Indian in his great-grandfather's tribe that dreamed he would travel five rivers from their beginning to their end. Everyone told him he shouldn't try it, that he'd never find his way back. But he said his dream was a very strong one, so the tribe built him a canoe that would be light enough to carry by himself and he started off. The journey took him three winters and four summers. He nearly froze to death and plenty of times he didn't have anything to eat but roots and wild berries. He had to hide from unfriendly tribes and he didn't know if he'd ever find his way back but he did and there was a big celebration for him and they changed his name to 'Wandering Bear.'"

Ernie was impressed. "You ought to write down some of your grandfather's stories, Nina. You could write them up for your school magazine. That's what I do."

Nina thought of the one-room schoolhouse she went to over on Resort Pike. There was no school magazine. Sometimes she didn't even have enough paper to do her lessons on. But how could she tell Ernie that? He didn't know what it was like to be poor. The things he and his sisters wanted were all *extra* things. Not things people really needed. They *had* those things. She didn't. And now when her father brought money home they were all afraid. They knew where it came from. If the Hemingways ever found out what her father was doing, they wouldn't let her work here.

Ernie was saying, "You could tell them to me and I could write them for you."

"What *you* can do," Ursula told him, "is carry this dishpan outside and dump the dishwater on Momma's rose bushes. She says the soapy water keeps the bugs away."

After the warm kitchen the yard was cool and airy. Ernie thought people were crazy to live in houses when they could live in tents. He wondered if Nina would be willing to live in a tent. The careful, almost loving way she dusted even their oldest pieces of furniture worried him. You couldn't have cherrywood chests and oak tables cluttering up a tent.

He scared a rabbit up in the yard and stood watching it move off into the woods. It made a quick leap and then it stood absolutely still under the illusion that if it were motionless it would be invisible. It took the rabbit several leaps and long pauses to reach the dark line of trees.

When Ernie got back to the kitchen, he found it empty. Nina was helping his mother put Leicester to bed and his sisters were deep in a discussion of what they were going to wear to the opera. Even Sunny had been drawn into an argument over a crucial question of whether or not their Panama straw hats with the streamers would be better than satin hair bows. No one bothered to ask his opinion. They didn't even see him leave.

Rowing back to his camp across the dark lake, Ernie wondered if a white man could ever know the land the way the Indians used to. You had to live close to the land and depend on it. Not for vegetables and fruit and fish like his family did, but for everything you ate and wore and lived in. When it had the power of life or death over you, that was when a person really knew the land.

7
Danger on the Dark Stream

The larva of the caddis fly has fragile gills and a tender stomach. To protect itself from becoming injured as it prowls about the bottom of the stream looking for food, it builds a little box around itself made of pebbles and grains of sand welded together with a gluelike substance. You can see it twitching along the river bottom packed into its stony suitcase.

The larva eats, outgrows its case, and makes a larger one. Finally it shuts itself up altogether and rests while its body begins to take a new shape. One night it breaks out of its case and becomes a caddis fly. On a summer evening hundreds of thousands of these flies may make their way to the surface of a stream. When that happens the trout rise to catch them and fishermen catch the trout.

In his dream Ernie was being jolted downhill by runaway horses. The carriage was shaking so he was sure he would be thrown. "Ernie, hey, Ernie! Wake up! You want to come? The hatch is on." Ted Lacour was shaking his cot.

"What time is it?" Ernie asked. He was still half asleep and time seemed to belong to someone else.

"It's nearly midnight. Let's get going. Every minute we waste is a fish we're not catching. That's money I lose. I can sell all the trout I catch to restaurants."

Ernie struggled into his shirt and trousers. He pulled on a pair of wool socks and stepped into his rubber boots. "Who's out there with you?" Now that his eyes were becoming used to the dark, he could make out a second shadowy figure.

"It's Nina. We came over together in our boat. She said you told her to come along but I sure don't know why. She's just going to be in our way. She'll stumble around in the water and scare off the trout."

"I won't," Nina said. "I can be just as quiet as you can."

"Sure she can," Ernie said. "Come on, let's go." He picked up his fishing gear. "My dad and I tied plenty of caddis flies this winter. I've got enough for all of us."

On the way to the stream, Ernie, copying Ted, was careful not to pay much attention to Nina who hung back on the path. He looked up to Ted because Ted knew so much about hunting and fishing. And Ted was his own boss. He didn't have to check in with his family all the time. Nobody hung up a dish towel in front of the Lacour cabin as a signal for Ted to drop everything and come running home. Even if he was happy because Nina had come along with them, he wasn't going to let on and have Ted start ridiculing him for wanting to spend his time with a girl.

"Guess who I caught going through my stuff?" Ernie asked. "Tommy Thrake. You better watch out. He knows someone's been shooting squirrels."

"Oh, him. I can hear him coming a mile away. He walks through the woods like a cow on snowshoes. Plenty of times I've sneaked up on him. What happened when you caught him?" There was an expectant pleasure in Ted's voice as though he were looking forward to hearing what Ernie had done to Thrake.

Ernie was tempted to make a story up about how he had given Tommy Thrake a good thrashing. But all he said was, "He won't be coming around my place again." Ernie wasn't sure that was true.

Ted chuckled, pleased at his own vision of Ernie pitching into Thrake. "He'd better not bother me or he'll be sorry."

"His dad could put you in jail for shooting squirrels," Nina told him.

"What do I care? I can find a way out of any jail they put me in," Ted boasted.

They reached the stream. In the darkness you could hear something that sounded like outsized raindrops pelting the water. They stood still for a minute listening. Ernie played his flashlight on the water. Thousands of caddis flies were swarming over the stream. The air was thick with them. Trout were jumping up out of the water gorging themselves on the flies. As the trout broke the surface of the water they made soupy plopping sounds. You could see the white of the trouts' bellies as they flipped back into the water. Ernie flicked off his flashlight. His hands were shaking with excitement. "Did you ever see so many darn trout in your life!" He wished his dad were there.

Nina was standing next to him. "How are we going to catch the fish when they've got so much to eat already?"

"You put a fake fly in there that looks like the caddis flies. They snap it up just like a real one," Ted said. "When they're crazy like this they don't care what they eat."

Working in the light of the flashlight, they greased their lines. Ernie used some special stuff of his father's that came from England. Ted was slathering on something that looked like bacon fat. They caught one of the caddis flies and examined it. "Looks like we ought to use a black caddis," Ernie said. "You want one of these?" He held out a carefully tied fly to Ted, who was knotting onto the end of his line something that looked like a piece of lint you'd find in an old bathrobe pocket.

Ted refused his offer, but Nina took one of Ernie's flies and tied it to her leader. "They're just like the real ones, Ernie. They're almost too nice to get all messed up." You had to rub grease on them so they would float on the water's surface like the real flies.

The three of them stepped into the stream. Ernie thought it was exciting when you left the land and began to walk along in the water. It wasn't a big miracle like

Jesus walking on the water, but it always seemed to him like at least a small miracle. He could feel the river's chill through his rubber boots and wondered how Nina and Ted could wade in the cold water with nothing but sneakers on their feet. The current was swift and you had to place your feet carefully to keep from stumbling on the slippery stones. If you made a wrong move you might find yourself slipping into a deep hole. In the darkness the danger was greater because you couldn't see the drop-offs. A few years before this same stream had carried thousands of logs from the lumber camps down to the lake, where they were loaded onto steamers and shipped all over the country. You could still find some of the logs wedged into the river bank.

Ted kept ahead of them. He fished the stream nearly every day to get trout to sell and knew every inch of it. "Don't move unless I tell you," he said. "There's a hole about ten feet from me." Ted was enjoying being in charge. Ernie knew that although he had boots and a good trout rod and fancy flies, it was Ted Lacour who would decide where they would fish.

"Keep far enough apart," Ted told them, "so we have plenty of room to cast. And fish from the middle of the stream so you don't get your line tangled in the trees."

Ernie could hear Nina's line whipping back and forth downstream from him. She sounded like she knew what she was doing. He didn't know any girls at the Oak Park high school who knew how to fish for trout.

In the dark Ernie couldn't see a thing. He was fishing

the stream by memory. But it was a different stream at night. In the daytime it had no secrets. You could see right down to the riverbed. At night you realized the river had a life of its own. The water sounded much louder as it rushed over the stones and logs. The stream smelled more pungent, too, damp and dank from the evening ground fogs. Though you couldn't see them, you knew there were night animals all around you: mink and beaver slipping silently by your legs or a raccoon at the water's edge washing its food or hunting for crayfish. Soft partings of the air told you bats were diving at the caddis flies. The trout, so stealthy in the daytime, were thrashing about all around him, making him feel as though he were witnessing some eerie ceremony.

"I got one," Ted called out in a whisper that barely carried over the water to Ernie. A few minutes later Ted pulled in a second one and then a third. Ernie felt embarrassed at the condescending way he had offered Ted one of his flies. He would have to get a closer look at what Ted was using so he could describe it to his dad. A second later he felt a quick jerk on his own line. He set the hook and played the fish, letting it take all the line it wanted. He could tell from the way it tugged that it was a good-sized one. His rod had been a Christmas present. It was light and beautifully balanced. He could feel every movement the fish made.

He waited until the trout was safely in his creel before he announced his success to Ted. Nina got the next trout. After that they were all pulling them in. The trout were the big lunkers that seldom came up to feed during the daytime, wary fish that had thrown away their usual caution in the excitement of seeing so much food.

All of a sudden the hatch was over and the trout disappeared into their nooks and niches behind logs and in the recesses of the banks. "We might as well take off," Ted called.

Ernie wanted one more fish. Then he would have as many as Ted. "Let's give it another ten minutes," he said.

"My feet are getting numb," Ted complained.

Ernie thought guiltily of his own feet comfortable in their wool socks and waterproof boots. "Three more casts," he pleaded. That was a lucky number. He aimed his first cast slightly downstream from the opposite bank. He had picked up two good ones there. He was retrieving the line when he felt something hard slide along his body. Startled, he jumped back, nearly losing his footing. It was there again—a sharp nudge and then nothing. He knew at once what it was: a deadhead log the current had worked lose from the bank. He had been lucky. The log had only grazed him. If it had caught him across the back, it would have knocked him over into the water. He swept the stream's surface with his flashlight. The log was already several feet ahead of him, riding the surface like a giant brown water snake. It was headed in Nina's direction.

"A deadhead!" he yelled. "Nina, look out. There's a log coming toward you." He stumbled over the slippery stones toward Nina, nearly stepping into a hole. There was no way he could move quickly and hang onto his trout rod and the flashlight. He hesitated a minute and then flung the rod toward the bank. Its lightness was hard to throw. He wasn't sure where it landed. The flashlight beam jerked back and forth from the stream to the woods as he tried to get to Nina. Ted was thrashing though the water from the other direction. He heard Nina call out but when he reached the place where she had been standing, there was nothing to see but the log sweeping on into the darkness.

"Ernie, keep your flashlight over here," Ted shouted to him.

He aimed the beam in the direction of Ted's voice. Ted rose from the water. "I must'a missed her." His face was a strange sulphur yellow in the light. His wet shirt clung shroudlike to his chest.

Ernie couldn't just stand there in the water, not doing anything. He made his way over to Ted and yanking off his boots he dove into the water, letting the current take him downstream. He knew Nina could swim. If she were all right she should be struggling to get back to them and answering their calls, but when they listened for her there was only silence. She might have hit her head. If she were unconscious the stream would have her, dragging her along with it. He had to move faster than the current and he had to sweep the stream from bank to bank so he wouldn't miss her.

Ernie thrust the flashlight at Ted. The right side of the river was shallow. Ted could cover it and still keep the flashlight trained on the water. Ernie kept to the left where it was deeper with sudden drop-offs. The current was so swift that it carried him off before he could probe the bottom and he had to fight his way back upstream and try again. The current was his enemy. It was worse than any boxing match he had ever been in. In boxing there were moments between rounds when you could relax your guard. His feet kept groping for the bottom. Sometimes it was there and he could fight against the stream. Then he'd hit a deep spot and his whole body would be swept off. He thought of Nina, maybe just inches ahead of him and being carried farther away. He had a frightening image of her floating helpless in the water, her hair streaming out on the surface like a giant black water lily.

The stream was changing direction. The shallow part was on the left now, and the deep part on the right. They reached a horseshoe bend where the stream circled around a narrow point of land. "Get out," he yelled to Ted. "Quick! We can cross the land, catch Nina on the other side."

Ted understood. The distance across the point was no more than a couple of hundred feet but by the stream it would be nearly a quarter of a mile. Maybe they could gain enough time to get ahead of Nina. They raced across the spit. It was low land, flat and boggy. The beam from the flashlight was getting dimmer. It hardly penetrated the darkness. With each step their feet sunk down and the porous ground sucked at them, holding them back.

Once Ernie stumbled over a cedar stump and fell down. It was like falling on a hundred wet smelly sponges. Finally they reached the water and plunged in.

"Grab my hand," Ernie yelled. Again Ted understood. The stream was narrow there. By holding hands they could span it, forming a human net. They began walking back upstream against the current, calling Nina's name.

From somewhere in the darkness they heard an answer. "Ted." For a second Ernie was hurt that it wasn't his name Nina had called. The feeling disappeared in the relief of hearing Nina's voice. They struggled against the current toward the sound.

"Nina, where are you?" Ernie called. The stream was widening again and they might miss her. Ernie felt her against him. He hung onto her harder than he had ever hung on to anything before. Her body was shaking from cold and fear. He took one arm. Ted had the other.

"The log," she said, hardly able to talk, but having to say what had happened, to get control of it with words. "It knocked me off my feet. When I tried to swim it was on top of me and I hit my head on it trying to get out from under it. I just went with the current. I don't remember where. Then it wasn't so deep anymore and I heard you."

They were out of the water now, but Nina was so limp they could hardly hold her up. She was crying softly.

Ted began to yell at Nina, "I told you not to come along. You're nothing but trouble. All the fishpoles gone. Know how much that costs? Plenty. And the trout. I was going to sell them. The whole damn night gone for nothing." His voice broke with frustration and disappointment.

Nina pulled away from them and headed into the woods. "Come on, Ted," Ernie said roughly, "let's get back to my camp and we can build a fire and dry off. You can't row home in those wet clothes." Ted had no business talking to Nina like that. The log wasn't her fault. Ernie felt Ted was blaming him for asking Nina to come along with them.

No one had anything to say on the way back. They were all thinking about what had happened and what had almost happened—weighing the one against the other. Ted, now that he had calmed down, could see there was more luck in Nina's being all right than bad luck in losing the trout.

A light wind touched their clothes, turning them into cold compresses. Once Ted, who was in the lead, stumbled against a tree stump and cursed. Ernie was wondering how he'd explain the loss of his trout rod to his father. His parents could be generous, but they expected you to take care of what they gave you.

Nina wasn't afraid anymore, only angry at Ted for yelling at her. She could do everything he could and nearly as well. But Ted never wanted her around. He kept her out of his world. Her mother had little time for her. Her father was was hardly ever home. At the Hemingways,

Ernie and his sisters did things together all the time. Sunny was always out fishing with Ernie and Sunny was only eleven. Maybe the Hemingways would take her to Oak Park with them when they went back in the fall. She would be a part of their family. She wouldn't care if she ever saw Ted and her parents again. She would miss her younger sister and brother but she would make a lot of money in Oak Park and she'd send them nice clothes and toys. She wondered if she could ask Ernie to talk his parents into taking her.

When they got to the camp the two boys built a fire. Nina tried to hand Ted some wood but he pushed it aside and selected his own pieces. Ernie brought out some blankets for them and then went into his tent to change his clothes. When he came back, Ted and Nina had wrapped themselves up in the blankets. Their wet clothes were hung on stakes around the fire, waving in the light wind like tired banners.

Ernie had to grin. Sitting there by the campfire with their angry faces and the blankets wrapped around them, Ted and Nina looked like the white man's image of the red man. Ted must have guessed what Ernie was thinking. He smiled, too. "Some powwow, huh?"

"I'll make some coffee for us." Ernie filled up the coffee pot with water and threw in a handful of coffee and some of the crushed egg shells he saved each morning from his breakfast. His dad said the egg shells kept the coffee clear. The boiling coffee smelled delicious. Ernie filled three baked bean cans and handed them around.

Ted was almost cheerful. "Hot damn," he said, "I never saw so many fish. They had plenty of fire in their tails. They just about jumped in my pocket. Wasn't that something Ernie? Don't worry about your trout rod. Nina can row back in the morning and look for the poles. Probably they're snagged on some log not more'n a mile or two downstream. Next time you won't go fishing with a girl, eh?"

Nina was staring into the fire. Her head was down and Ernie couldn't see her face. "She caught as many fish as we did," he said. He didn't care what Ted thought of him.

"You think she's so good you can have her," Ted laughed. "We trade. You give me your trout pole, I give you Nina. She's no good to us anymore." His voice was bitter. "She works over at your house all the time. Then she comes home and she says to my ma, 'You do it this way. That's how the Hemingways do it.' Or she's whining, 'I gotta have this or that, all the Hemingway girls have one.' We're sick of that. You just keep her."

Nina had drawn the blanket tighter, trying to disappear into it. "You talk too much, Ted," she said in an angry voice. "Everything that comes into your head falls right out of your mouth."

Ernie saw she was embarrassed. "What's the matter with her wanting to better herself?" he asked.

"Better herself?" Ted said scornfully. "What makes you think being like your dumb sisters would make her better? Can they run a trap line or tan hides or skin a deer? My sister is smarter than all your sisters put together. Why else does your mother have to pay Nina to come work for her when she's got four girls who could help her?"

Ernie started to say that his sisters did help with the work and that Sunny could fish as well as Nina could and what use would running a trap line be in Oak Park, but he could see Nina was looking pleased at what Ted had said about her. Ernie kept quiet.

Ted relented. "Even if your sisters can't do much, they're plenty nice looking. I wouldn't mind having one." His laughter was suggestive.

Ernie was furious. He started for Ted but Ted reached for his clothes and disappeared still laughing behind the tent.

Nina looked apologetically at Ernie. "Ted doesn't mean what he says." She picked up her clothes and was heading for the darkness beyond the fire.

"You can change your clothes in my tent," Ernie told her. He felt his cheeks burning.

With a quick look in the direction Ted had gone, Nina whispered, "You won't tell your ma the things Ted said?"

"Heck, no."

"She might not want me back."

"She likes you, Nina. We all do," he added, stumbling over the words.

Nina slipped into his tent. Ernie waited outside trying not to think about what was going on inside. He was used to seeing his sisters running around the house in their camisoles and petticoats. He never gave it a second thought. But Nina was different. He got up and was poking furiously at the fire when he heard a thrashing in the woods. Why was Ted making so much noise? A flashlight swept over the tent and stopped at Ernie's face. His eyes were blinded. He tried to move out of the glare. At that moment Nina came out of the tent.

The flashlight was running toward him. A man stepped into the campfire's circle of light. It was Nina's father. Ernie started to say something to him but Mr. Lacour grabbed him and started shaking him. Ernie thought the world had gone crazy.

"What do you think you doing with my girl! I kill you!" Mr. Lacour twisted Ernie's arm behind his back.

Ernie tried to struggle free, but each movement caused knives of pain to shoot through his arm. He heard Nina screaming and felt her throw herself at her father. The next minute Ted was there.

"We were fishing," Ted was shouting. "We were just fishing and we got wet and had to dry our clothes." Nina was on the ground sobbing.

Mr. Lacour looked around, disbelief on his face, but he let Ernie go. "You tell me where fish and poles are? *Vite!*" In his anger he reverted to the French word. He grabbed Ted and gave him a shove. "It better be the truth or you'll be plenty sorry."

"There was a hatch on and we were fishing. Then a log came along and knocked Nina over into the water and she nearly drowned only Ernie saved her. She would'a drowned if it wasn't for Ernie. He lost his fishing pole—and I lost mine and my fish, too," he had to add.

Mr. Lacour yanked Nina to her feet. "Is your brother telling the truth?"

"Yes," Nina sobbed, "yes."

Mr. Lacour gave Ernie a long look and then turned to Ted and Nina. "You two get into the boat and get home fast. I never want to see you here. Not anywheres near here. Nina, you got no business going fishing. That's for men."

Ernie watched Nina and Ted hurry down to their boat. He was alone with Mr. Lacour. He wondered if he should run. Only Mr. Lacour was right next to him. Close enough to grab him again if he made a move. For a wild minute Ernie thought he might throw himself at Mr. Lacour but the man weighed twice as much as he did. In the firelight his face was all dark shadows. Ernie kept still.

"I tell you somethin'." Mr. Lacour's face was close to his. Ernie could see his narrowed eyes staring at him. "You'd be a damn smart boy to pack up all your junk and get out of here. You got a house. You go there."

Ernie thought of the book that had been torn apart and the damage to his campsite. He suddenly felt afraid.

Mr. Lacour must have seen the fear. "That's right.

You know I'm not fooling." He gave Ernie a last long look, turned and strode off into the woods.

Ernie wondered if he ought to get out right away. But even Mr. Lacour wouldn't expect him to break camp in the middle of the night. Besides, he was so tired he could hardly move. He made himself go into his tent without looking over his shoulder toward the woods where Mr. Lacour had disappeared. He threw himself down on the cot and pulled the blanket over his shoulders. He was shivering. It was the blanket Nina had around her. He tried not to think about Nina. It was true what Ted had said. She had caused a lot of trouble. If Ted hadn't been there to explain, Mr. Lacour would probably have beaten him up into matchsticks. He couldn't forget that Mr. Lacour had suspected him and Nina. The more he thought about that, the more embarrassed he got. He had to admit that even if he wouldn't ever *do* anything like that, he had thought about it. His father would say that was just as bad.

Once he and Marce had read the whole King James Bible, all 1,264 pages, for a contest at church. They had read day and night for weeks. It was written the way he imagined God would talk to you if, God forbid, he ever should. Ernie's thoughts about Nina reminded him of a part from the sermon on the mount that said, "Whosoever looketh on a woman to lust after her hath committed adultery with her already in his heart." He wasn't exactly sure what adultery was. He had tried once to discuss stuff like that with his dad and had been told it wasn't the sort of thing decent people talked about. When he was with other boys he didn't like to ask any questions. That would give away how dumb he was.

He punched his pillow and turned over. Still, he couldn't stop his thoughts about Nina. Finally he gave up and drifted back to sleep with the image of Nina's warm soft body leaning over him, her long dark hair brushing his face like the soft black wing of some gentle bird.

8
The Blue Heron

"Ernie?" It was Nina's voice. He thought he was still dreaming. Then he saw it was morning.

"Nina?" He hurried out of the tent. Nina had his trout rod. She was wearing a pair of Ted's old overalls rolled up to her knees and a heavy sweater he thought he had remembered seeing on Ted. The clothes were too large for her and made her look like a child.

"Where did you find my trout rod?" He could hardly believe his good luck. He would have to take the reel apart right away and oil it so it wouldn't rust.

"It was snagged on a log. About a mile down from—you know."

Ernie saw the memory of what had almost happened to her was still frightening. She couldn't bring out the words: a mile down from where I nearly drowned.

"I hope it's not spoiled," she said.

Ernie forgot about his pleasure in seeing the trout rod again. While he had been sleeping, Nina had rowed all the way across the lake and gone back to that awful place and back into the water. He started to thank her but she shook her head.

"It was my fault you lost it. Listen, Ernie, I've got to get away from home. I know there's gonna be trouble."

"What kind of trouble?"

"I can't tell," Nina said. "Anyhow, they're always fighting and now Pa's mad at me because of last night. Can't you get your ma and pa to take me back to Oak Park with them?"

Ernie wasn't so sure but he promised, "I'll talk to them. My dad's coming tomorrow. Nina . . ."

She waited.

"If they don't, you and I could run away and get married."

"But you're only sixteen and I'm not even that."

"Well, we look older. We could go somewhere where they don't know us."

"How could we live? You don't have a job."

"There's lots of things I could do." He was going to name them, but none came to mind. He thought of the vegetable garden there at Longfield. "We've got more produce than we need. I can sell some of it to the resorters. Sunny and I made a lot of money doing that last year. Anyhow it would give us enough to get away on."

Nina looked uncertain.

"Then I could get a job as a reporter."

"Could we live near a city? I've never seen one except Petoskey and that's not very big."

"Sure we could."

Nina looked like she wanted to believe him. "I've got to get back now. Ursula's taking care of the baby for me." Before she left she put a hand on his arm. "Ernie, I heard Pa tell Ted you better move your camp away from here. He was plenty mad. I know he meant it." She turned away and disappeared into the woods.

Ernie had been thinking hard about how Mr. Lacour had told him to clear out. Last night he had thought he would, but this morning in the bright August sunlight he decided he'd wait until tomorrow when his dad could tell him what to do.

Thinking of his dad he decided he'd better catch up on his chores. Ernie wanted him to be in a good mood when he asked him to take Nina back to Oak Park. The last time Ernie had been in the potato field it was crawling with bugs. He knew the bugs had multiplied because he had spent too much time reading and not enough time tending the garden. Working alone it would take him all day to pick the potato bugs off the plants.

He tied his red shirt to a tall birch at the edge of the lake. It was a signal he had worked out with Sunny. He was still on his first row of potatoes when she appeared, out of breath from the run up the beach. "I had to finish shaking out the rugs before I could get away. Did you know in Japan you can't come into the house unless you take your shoes off? Are we going fishing?"

"I'll take you fishing this afternoon if you'll help me pick off the potato bugs."

"Ugh! I hate the way they hang onto the plants with their feet. Can we have a picnic, too?" Sunny knew she had some bargaining power.

"Yes, but we've got to get them all." He handed her a coffee can with kerosene in it. "Drop the bugs into the can and the kerosene'll kill them."

"At least we don't have to squash each one. How come you're after the bugs all of a sudden? Because Dad's coming tomorrow?"

"Partly. Partly because we have to start selling some of this stuff like we did last year. I've got to get some money."

"What do you need money for?"

"None of your beeswax."

It was noon when they finished. The August day had grown still and bright white with heat. Sun flooded the sky. They were covered with sweat and their shoulders and arms were burned to a red tenderness. Their legs ached from stooping. The fumes from the kerosene had made them giddy. While picking off the bugs, Ernie had been thinking of what he had promised Nina. He hoped his parents would agree to take her back to Oak Park. If they didn't he'd have to marry her and the idea of getting married scared him a lot. Even Sunny's profuse apologies to the potato bugs as she dropped them in the kerosene can hadn't cheered him.

When they finished they packed slabs of bread and hunks of cheese along with radishes and green onions from the garden. Sunny's contribution to the picnic was a thick wedge of angel food cake sneaked from the pantry.

Before they got into the boat they splashed each other to cool off. Walloon Lake was perfectly smooth in the still air. The drops of water from the spray seemed to hang in the air for a moment or two before falling back into the lake. The water felt so good that they both plunged in, clothes and all. Ernie wondered if he would have a good time like that with Nina if they got married. He guessed that after you had a wife things were pretty serious all the time. He felt a little panicky. If he married Nina he wouldn't be able to finish school or go off to the war like he wanted to. He wouldn't be coming back to Longfield to camp out next summer. He began to feel depressed again.

Sunny was wringing the water out of her long blond hair. "We finished our new bathing suits," she said. "We wanted to have them done before Dad comes. They've got sailor collars and puffed sleeves. If Momma hadn't said we had to make the skirts way down to our knees, they'd look real nice." Sunny paused. "Ernie, look. Who's that up on the bank?"

"Tommy Thrake. He's always hanging around." Tommy hurried into the woods. Since Ernie had found out it wasn't Thrake who messed up his stuff, he didn't pay too much attention to him.

As they were getting into the boat Ernie said, "Wait a minute." He climbed up the hill to his tent and brought back his gun. In case Thrake was still hanging around, Ernie didn't want him to think he was intimidated.

Sunny looked surprised. "Dad said you shouldn't carry your gun unless you have a good reason."

"I know what I'm doing and you don't have to go and blab to him."

Sunny was hurt. "I've never snitched on you." She would have died first.

Ernie was sorry for talking to her like that. More than once his parents had warned him to control his temper. It was just that everything was piling up on him. To make up for yelling at her, he headed the boat toward a part of the lake Sunny liked.

"We're going to my favorite spot, aren't we?" She knew it was Ernie's way of apologizing.

"Yeah, we should get some bass there." It was a deserted stretch of beach. Fallen trees extended out into the water along the shoreline, creating hiding places for fish. There weren't many places like that left on the lake. From nearly everywhere else you could see cottages or one of the hotels. From this place you could look into a thick tangle of trees where birds and animals or anything else could look out at you without you seeing them. Muskrats slipped through the water and disappeared into the dark recesses of the bank, and ducks slid silently by, trailing a string of ducklings.

They let the boat drift along the bank so the motion of their oars wouldn't spook the fish, neither one of them saying a word. They moved so silently that a row of snapping turtles sunning themselves on a log like a row of overturned saucers didn't even notice them.

Ernie reached for his gun, his eye on a big turtle with its head out on a log like a dog resting his chin on his master's foot. A big snapper like that could bite a man's finger off. They ate a lot of fish eggs, too. He raised his gun and aimed. Then something so still that he hadn't noticed it started up at the movement of his arm and swept into the air, enormous wings pumping, legs dangling, long neck folded back between its shoulders. It was a great blue heron. You saw a heron sometimes stalking fish along the shore, folding a long yellow leg up at the knee, pausing for a moment and then placing it down with great care before raising the other leg. It stepped methodically along, extending its neck and then drawing it back like a cobra swaying to music. Suddenly the great bird would freeze and faster than you could see, it would spear a fish or a frog with the sword of its bill.

Impulsively Ernie swung the gun up and pulled the trigger. The bird hovered for a second in midair and then fell out of the sky as though it had suddenly forgotten the secret of flight.

Ernie climbed over the boat's edge into the shallow water and waded toward the floating bird. When he reached it he held it up by its legs like a huge dead chicken for Sunny to see.

Sunny knew Ernie was waiting for her to applaud the kill but she couldn't bring herself to say a word. The great grayish-blue bird was nearly as large as she was. Could you treat it as just another bird?

Ernie swung the heron into the boat. "Wait'll Dad

sees it. He can stuff it for his collection." Ernie tried to make his voice sound excited, but it didn't come off. The two of them peered down at the bird. Its long wings were the slate blue of Lake Michigan ice. Its head and throat were snow white. There were black patches on either shoulder like a soldier's epaulets. Over each eye a black streak ended in a narrow plume of black feathers. A trickle of blood was seeping from its bill.

Ernie and Sunny stared silently at the bird. It was impossible to imagine that soft inert pile of feathers stuffed and lifelike again. Ernie felt as if his father were looking over his shoulder. It gave him a sinking feeling. He arranged the bird gently under the back seat of the boat so it would be out of the sun and out of sight of anyone who might happen on the boat. He wasn't too anxious to look at it anymore. "We may as well go find a place for our picnic. It'll give the fish a chance to settle down. I roiled up the water plenty going after the heron."

Sunny wanted to tell Ernie not to feel badly but he was pretending he felt all right so she couldn't.

"Too hot to sit down here on the sand," Ernie said. "We'll go up into the woods."

"Are you going to take your gun?" Sunny asked warily. She hoped he wouldn't kill anything else that day.

"No. It'll be safe in the boat. No one's around."

The woods were cool, and sitting in the green filtered light of the bushy hemlocks they took their time about eating. Neither one of them was anxious to get back to the dead bird. But when they returned to the boat the blue heron was gone. Their first response was to look overhead, half believing the bird had revived and might be flying menacingly over them, its sharp beak ready to take a cruel revenge. The sky was empty.

"Why would someone want to steal a dead bird?" Sunny asked. "They didn't even take your gun."

"I don't know. It doesn't make sense. If someone catches them with it they could get arrested and sent to jail."

"You mean if someone caught *you* with it *you* could go to jail?"

"Sure." He tried to sound nonchalant but the word "jail" gave him a funny feeling. What if Tommy Thrake had seen him go back to his tent for his gun and then followed them along the shore? What if he had been right there when he shot the heron? And now Thrake had the evidence. He had been stupid to leave the heron in the boat. Once his father had driven him and his sisters all the way to Joliet where the Illinois state prison was. He had pointed out the foreboding walls and told them in a stern voice that they would end up there if they disobeyed their parents. "Listen," Ernie said, his heart sinking, "we've got to get back to Windemere fast."

"How come?"

"Don't ask questions. Save your breath for rowing."

But they were too late. Marce was waiting on the dock for them. Her glance traveled quickly from their worried faces to Ernie's gun. "Then you *did* do it," she said. "The game warden, Thrake, and his son were here about five minutes ago. They came to arrest you for killing a blue heron."

"What blue heron?" Ernie asked.

Sunny's mouth fell open.

"What's your gun doing in the boat?" Marce stared hard at him.

"I was just going to shoot a couple of snapping turtles." He couldn't bear to admit what he had done to Marce. She made a point of never getting into trouble.

"Tommy Thrake found the heron in *your* boat, Ernie."

"Well, someone must have put it there."

"Ernie, I don't believe a word you're saying and God will punish you for lying."

He gave in, ashamed to have Sunny a witness to his lie. "Is Momma angry?"

"She's just as angry at the Thrakes as she is at you. They came pounding on our door wanting to talk to Dad. When she told them he wasn't coming until tomorrow, they started asking her a lot of questions about you and telling how they were going to put you in jail and every-thing. They sounded really pleased with themselves. They even wanted to borrow the launch to go after you but Momma said we didn't lend it to strangers. They were hanging around on the front porch waiting for you until Momma told them to get out. They went but said they'd be back."

Sunny looked more frightened with every word. "Ernie, what'll you do?"

He wished his dad were there, even if he had to put

up with a lecture. He didn't want to face the Thrakes when they returned. He could imagine the way Tommy Thrake would gloat. He certainly didn't want to go to jail. There was no point in heading back to his camp. It would be the first place they would look for him. But he had to go someplace. "I can hide out at the Dilworths'." Now that he had a plan of action and someplace to go, he felt a little better. In fact he was beginning to feel excited, as if he were having some sort of adventure.

"I want to go with you," Sunny said.

"You'll do no such thing," Marce told her. "Mamma'd have a fit."

"But I was *there* when he shot the heron." Sunny felt cheated.

"That's OK, kid," Ernie said. "I may have to take off and hide in the woods." He made his voice sound deep and serious. "Maybe I'll have to be away a long time. You're better off here." He turned to Marce. "What if they find my boat on the beach near the trail to Horton Bay? They'll know where I've gone."

"I'll take you across the lake and then bring the boat back," she said, "But we'll have to hurry."

As she left Ernie on the opposite shore, Marce promised, "The minute it's safe for me to get away, I'll bring you some clothes and money. Good luck," she called.

For the first time in a long while Ernie felt close to Marce. She was helping him when she knew people could be arrested for aiding and abetting a criminal. She's a good sport, he thought to himself.

As he began the three-mile hike to Horton Bay, he started to feel a little scared. What if he had to hide out forever? He'd never see Nina or his family again. He let himself think about that, enjoying the sadness of it. He imagined traveling across the country from one forest to another, each more remote than the one before. He would live with the Indians and there would be a price on his head and posters of him in all the post offices with a big sign above his picture: "Wanted for Shooting a Blue Heron." That didn't sound right. Maybe it would just say "fugitive."

Before too long he would be able to grow a beard. Then no one would recognize him. He'd pick an Indian name for himself. Something like, "He Who Walks Alone." Someday he'd come back to Windemere. He saw himself walking into the cottage and surprising everyone. His parents would be old and frail (although it was a little hard to picture his mother that way) and his sisters all grown up. They'd be married with kids, except Sunny, who would have sworn she wouldn't marry until he returned. And Nina. Nina would be waiting for him.

By the time he reached Horton Bay he was feeling a lot better. He had almost forgotten what he had done and was only thinking that if they were making all this fuss over him, he must be important. He looked around carefully, expecting to see a posse waiting there for him. But in the quiet summer afternoon the town was deserted. He skirted a couple of houses and peered out from a tree or two. Then he made a dash for the blacksmith shop. Luckily Uncle Jim Dilworth was all alone soldering a patch on what looked like Aunty Beth's big tin tea kettle.

"Well, Ernie, I didn't expect to have the pleasure of your company. Sit yourself down."

"I can't, Uncle Jim. I got to keep moving. Someone's after me." Ernie tried to sound desperate.

"Oh? Well, I dare say between the two of us we can fend them off. I got an iron skillet or two here we could use. Many's the time your Aunty Beth showed me how to wield one." He grinned at his joke.

Ernie felt resentful. He had expected to be taken seriously. He tried again. "I really *am* in trouble. The game warden's after me."

"You mean Thrake? If that son of a gun's looking for you, you *have* got trouble. He'd turn his own mother in for killing the Christmas goose. What'd you do?"

For a minute Ernie couldn't answer the simple question. He had been so caught up with the excitement of being chased that he had lost sight of what really *had* happened. He wished they were after him for doing something noble like killing a wolf while it was eating someone up. Uncle Jim was looking at him, waiting for an answer. "I shot a blue heron."

"Well, Ernie, if I say so myself, that wasn't too smart a thing to do. That's a mighty pretty bird."

Ernie was silent. He wished he had stayed in the woods.

"What happened? The bird come after you?" It was the first time Ernie had ever heard the cutting edge of sarcasm in Jim Dilworth's voice.

"No, sir. Me and Sunny were fishing and I saw this big snapping turtle. I was just going to shoot it when the blue heron flew up and I turned the gun on the heron instead. I thought my dad would like to have it for his stuffed bird collection." He couldn't seem to put much conviction in his voice.

"You always were a little trigger-happy, Ernie. As for a stuffed heron, I don't know that your ma would be too happy with a bird three feet high stuck on top of her piano or maybe peeking down from the mantelpiece."

Ernie knew Jim Dilworth was not an unkind man. He guessed his Uncle Jim hadn't thought much of the cocky way he had come walking into the smithy. All of Ernie's swagger left him. He was close to tears.

"What're you figuring to do, Ernie?" The gruffness was gone from Jim Dilworth's voice.

"I guess I better run away."

"Just where you figuring to run to?"

"I don't know." Living in the woods for the rest of his life no longer seemed like such a good idea.

"I'll tell you what, Ernie. I know Judge Stroud over in Boyne City. He and his wife been over for a couple of Aunty Beth's Sunday dinners. He's a pretty good sort. I'll hitch the wagon up and we'll drive over there."

"You mean I have to give myself up?" It had never occurred to him that he would be face to face with a judge.

"Well, if Thrake gets hold of you, you could end up with a jail sentence and your name in the paper. Those deer poachers are just about driving him crazy. He'll want to take it out on someone. But if the judge is in a good mood, you could get off with a fine. I don't see you got any other choice. You ready?"

"Yes, sir."

On the ride over Uncle Jim kept up a friendly stream of conversation, but Ernie wasn't listening. He was trying to figure out what the word "mitigating" meant. He knew people were sometimes let off for crimes they committed if there were mitigating circumstances. Was his worrying about Nina a mitigating circumstance? Or the potato bugs? Or the heat? Or Mr. Lacour pushing him around last night? He had to admit that what might be a mitigating circumstance for him might not seem like one to the judge.

The hearing took place, not in the judge's private office as he had hoped, but right out in public in the courtroom. An American flag stood in one corner of the courtroom and the flag of the state of Michigan in the other. A picture of President Wilson frowned down at him from the wall. Two or three courtroom loungers were stretched out on benches, passing the time of day. When they saw Ernie ushered in by Jim Dilworth they sat up, pleased that there was to be a little performance to break up their boredom.

Ernie had expected Judge Stroud would be old with a white beard and look a little like he imagined God looked. Instead the judge was a young man. He appeared plenty serious, though, as if he didn't want anyone to think that because he was young they were going to be allowed to get away with anything. The judge listened impassively to Ernie's story. "You plead guilty?" he asked when Ernie had finished.

Ernie nodded.

"Speak up, boy. The clerk can't write down what your head does." One of the loungers laughed out loud. The judge slammed down the gavel, making Ernie jump.

Ernie repeated the awful words: "I plead guilty."

"You ever been in trouble with the law before?" the judge asked.

"No, sir."

"Don't you have something to do to keep yourself from getting into mischief?"

"I take care of my parents' vegetable garden and orchard." Being in a courtroom in front of the judge and the American flag and the picture of President Wilson had the effect of making Ernie scrupulously honest. So he added, "I fish a little, too. And read."

The judge looked interested. "What are you reading?"

"*Ivanhoe* and Theodore Roosevelt's book about Africa."

"So you like books. You ever hear what Roosevelt had to say about shooting something that's rare—like a blue heron?"

"No, sir."

"Roosevelt said that when he heard about the destruction of some rare species he felt just as if all the works of some great writer had perished."

Ernie felt terrible and he hated the judge for making him feel that way.

"I'll let you off with a fine this time," Judge Stroud said. "Fifteen dollars or fifteen days in jail."

Ernie's heart sank. All he had with him was a dollar and fifty cents. He'd have to go to jail after all. He saw the gray walls of the prison at Joliet closing in on him.

"Your honor," Jim Dilworth was saying, "I'll pay the boy's fine." He took three five-dollar bills out of his wallet. Ernie knew Jim Dilworth didn't usually carry that kind of money with him. He must have gotten it when he went for the wagon, knowing a fine would have to be paid.

On the way back to Horton Bay, Ernie promised, "I'll get the money from my dad and pay you back, Uncle Jim."

"I have a hunch your dad is going to tell you to earn it yourself."

Ernie was silent. He had thought he could make some money for himself and Nina. Now he owed more than he could ever make from selling the vegetables.

"Your Aunty Beth is lookin' for a regular supply of trout for the restaurant. Mr. Lacour used to supply us, but he's got other fish to fry. No pun intended." He grinned. "You're a pretty good fisherman, Ernie. How about you getting us some?"

"I could get 'em all right, but it's illegal to sell trout."

Ernie thought he wouldn't like to end up in a courtroom again.

Jim Dilworth gave Ernie a wink. "Let's just say you'll be making us a present of them." He gave a quick snap of the reins to hurry the horses. "Well, Ernie, I guess you learned your lesson today, eh?"

"Yes, sir," Ernie said. But thinking about Uncle Jim's arrangement with the trout, he wasn't sure just what lesson he had learned.

One thing was sure. He was glad the summer was almost over. The story about the heron would be all over town. The sooner he got away, the better. He almost hoped his parents wouldn't take Nina home with them. Then he and Nina could go someplace where no one had even heard of blue herons.

Remembering his dad would be arriving the next day, Ernie tried to piece together a story that would explain why he shot the heron. But it was no use. His dad's keen black eyes would see though it. He guessed he would tell the truth. His dad would be angry but not as angry as he would be if Ernie were to lie to him.

Ernie forced the heron out of his mind by thinking, instead, of the fishing he and his dad would be doing. The nights were cooling off and the trout were more active. Ernie couldn't resist saying, "I'll get you all the trout you want, Uncle Jim. My dad's coming tomorrow and he can help."

Jim Dilworth shot a quick look at Ernie. "Let's just keep it between ourselves, Ernie," he said.

9

The Burning Woods

Ernie stood just inside the screen door, breathing in the sharp vinegar-sugar smell of pickling syrup. He surveyed the organized mess his father was making of the kitchen. Glass jars stood waiting with open mouths on the counters. Vegetables in various stages of preparation lay in green heaps on the big wooden table. Dr. Hemingway had just arrived two days ago and already he was attacking a pile of onions with vigorous strokes of a long, wicked-looking knife while tears streamed down his face and disappeared into his beard. As he sliced away he dispatched a steady stream of orders to Ernie's sisters and Nina: "Ursula, try to chop those peppers a little finer. Nina, are you getting all the peel off the cukes? Sunny, wash out that kettle for me, will you, dear? Marce, if you don't stop your daydreaming you'll let the syrup boil over."

He was the general and the girls his troops. They all helped, but when the long columns of jars were filled with bread and butter pickles and marshaled into neat rows on the pantry shelves, the credit would go to Dr. Hemingway. It was a little family scheme to encourage him to produce the good-tasting preserves they would take back with them to Oak Park—the raspberry and blackberry jam, the apple jelly and piccalilli and cinnamon flavored applesauce. When they consumed the treats in the middle of the raw Illinois winter, they would think of Windemere and Walloon and know that there had been a summer and that it would come again.

"Ernie, how about giving us a hand?" his father asked.

Ernie stayed where he was. "The wood for the stove is getting low," he said. "I better go split some." The truth was he hated seeing his dad fussing around the kitchen wearing one of his mother's red checked dish towels like an apron and doing what Ernie thought ought to be women's work. His mother stayed out of the kitchen. She said the fumes from the boiling pickles gave her a headache.

"When are we going to go fishing?" he complained to his father. He was getting desperate to get his dad away from the house so he could talk to him about Nina going back to Oak Park with them.

"Well, Ernie, the cucumbers are just the right size for pickling. And you know yourself I had to get the tomatoes done yesterday. They were a little soft as it was." Ernie had watched Dr. Hemingway thoughtfully prod each big red fruit as though it were a patient requiring a careful diagnosis. "I would think that instead of bellyaching, you would pitch in. *Marce!* Wake up! The syrup is boiling over!"

Ernie turned away sullenly, purposely forgetting to close the screen door tightly. The flies would be attracted by the food smells and find their way into the kitchen. His dad hated flies. Ernie walked by the woodpile without giving it a glance. For weeks he had been saddled with his mother and his sisters. Now when his dad had finally come, he was spending all his time puttering around the kitchen like some old lady. Ernie kicked a stone, bruising his toe and making himself even angrier.

He tried to concentrate on what a good shot his dad was and all the stuff he knew about the outdoors, but Ernie kept picturing him in the kitchen with all the girls around him like bunch of handmaidens. What must Nina think? *Her* dad certainly didn't hang around the kitchen cooking up batches of pickles. Ernie'd never let Nina see *him* standing around hacking up little bits of vegetables or hanging over the stove.

He headed for the beach. It hadn't rained in over two weeks. For the last two days rain clouds had hung suspended in the sky but nothing had happened. The grass under his feet was more brown than green. The leaves on the alder bushes rustled like paper and even the moss on the tree trunks had a crisp look. Already an occasional yellow leaf detached itself from one of the maple trees and drifted to the ground. Fall was coming and nothing was working out right. His dad hadn't been in the house ten minutes when he had heard all about the blue heron.

"Jim Dilworth paid Ernie's fine," his mother had said. "We'll have to pay him back."

"We'll reimburse Jim, certainly," his father agreed, "but Ernie will have to pay us back. He deserved every penny of that fine. Ernie, how could anyone who cares as much as you do about the outdoors do a thoughtless thing like that? I have half a notion to take your gun away for the rest of the summer."

Ernie had flushed. He hated being reprimanded in front of his sisters, especially Marce, who looked smug, and Sunny, who looked miserable. He knew his father would never carry out the threat of taking his gun away. That was just talk to impress his mother. His mother always said his dad wasn't "firm" enough with him.

Then he had made the mistake of telling his dad about Mr. Lacour's threat, sure his dad would tell him to stay at Longfield. He even expected his father might get after Mr. Lacour for making the threat. Instead, Dr. Hemingway had said, "Well, Ernie, the summer's almost over. You might as well pack up your gear and come home."

When Ernie had protested, Dr. Hemingway had shrugged his shoulders. "Mr. Lacour and I have tangled a few times. He's not a man to cross. He can be unpleasant."

"Unpleasant! He's a bully. You should hear the way he yells at Mrs. Lacour and his kids. He needs to be taught a lesson."

"I gather you weren't quite so aggressive when Mr. Lacour was there. Now you want me to fight your battle for you. I'm not a fighting man, Ernie. Mr. Lacour probably resents our owning so much property over there. He used to hunt on that land before we bought it. I suppose he thinks he has prior rights. With a war going on in Europe and our country talking about joining in, it looks like we'll have all the fighting we need."

Ordinarily Ernie would have badgered his father. When you did that, either one of two things happened. He gave in or he got angry and they had a big tangle and Ernie lost and had to apologize and slink around the house for a day or two. Your chances were about fifty-fifty. But Ernie couldn't risk it. He had to keep on his dad's good side because there was something he had to ask him.

A couple of days ago he had found Nina sitting all hunched up in back of the tool shed, crying. Her long hair hung like two black curtains screening her face but he could see her shoulders shaking. Alarmed, he crouched down beside her. "Nina, what's the matter?" He touched her hand. It was wet with tears. He felt a sudden tenderness for her and a wonder you feel for a small wild animal, one you think you have tamed until you touch it and feel its heart pounding with fear.

"I thought you were going to ask your ma and pa if they'd take me with them." She turned a resentful face toward him. Her eyes were red and swollen and there were smudges on her cheeks where she had wiped away tears. Her voice was angry. Ernie knew it was because she didn't want anyone to see how hurt she was. She probably hated him for being there.

"You don't know what it's like," she told him, "to come here every day from my house. Your sisters have nice clothes. Marce has *two* pairs of shoes to wear just to parties. Your pa talks to your ma. They sit down and talk about things. Last night I heard him ask her if she wanted to go for a row on the lake with him. My pa never talks to my ma. He *tells* her. She never says anything. She gets more and more quiet. But the way she looks is terrible. And at night she sleeps with a knife under her pillow. What does she want a knife for? I don't want to stay there anymore. If your family won't take me to Oak Park, I'll get someone to marry me and have my own place to live."

"I told you I'd marry you." Ernie put an arm around Nina, holding her against him. For a minute she let her body go limp and he felt her warmth and slight weight against him. But the next minute Nina pulled away.

"You're just a kid. You go around peddling beans and potatoes and live in a tent. If you married me your folks would kick you out and you wouldn't even have a place to live and nothing to sell."

"I could get a job on a farm."

"I don't want to live on some old farm. I want to live in a city. If your folks won't take me to Oak Park I can marry Jimmy Powter. He wants to go to Detroit and work in an automobile factory. He says he can make plenty of money there."

"Jimmy Powter's too old for you!" Powter was an Indian who worked as a bark peeler. In the wintertime he ran a trap line. He must have been twenty-five. Ernie would die before he let Nina marry Jimmy Powter.

Ernie tackled his parents the next day. Unexpectedly, his mother agreed to the idea of taking Nina back to Oak Park with them.

"I'm not sure but what that wouldn't be a good idea, Ed. She's a willing little thing and awfully good with the baby."

"I don't think she's sixteen yet," his father objected. "She ought to stay here and finish school. Maybe next summer."

"Next summer will be too late," Ernie protested.

His father gave him a sharp look. "What do you mean, too late?"

"Well, her folks are fighting all the time. She hates it at home. She might run away or . . ." Ernie stopped himself.

"Or what, Ernie?" his father insisted.

"Nothing."

His parents exchanged knowing glances. "Perhaps your father is right after all," his mother said.

After that, no matter how much Ernie pleaded, they wouldn't change their minds. He thought if he could get his father out of the darn kitchen and off alone he could tell him how things were between him and Nina.

A pale gray haze lay over the hills. At first Ernie

thought it was some sort of fog. Then he noticed the sharp stinging smell of smoke. He wondered if someone was burning over their land to clear it of weeds. Only that was usually done in the springtime. He watched the haze form itself into big white swirls and mingle with the rain clouds.

All at once Ernie knew what it was and that he ought to do something right away. Tell someone. He stayed on watching, savoring the excitement of being the only one at Windemere to know. The one who would spread the news. Seconds went by before he sprang to his feet and ran for the cottage shouting, "Forest fire! Hey! It's a forest fire!"

"A fire! Where?" His father had been ladling pickles from a kettle into a jar. Now he held the ladle out in mid-air. "Where, Ernie?"

"In the direction of the Indian camp. The whole sky's full of smoke!"

Dr. Hemingway looked quickly around the kitchen as though he were considering how he might take it with him. Then he ripped off his towel and headed for the door, pausing long enough to hand the ladle, still full of pickles, to Marce.

"I'm coming with you," Ernie said.

"Me, too," Sunny pulled her hands out of the dishpan and shook the suds off onto the floor.

"Sunny," Dr. Hemingway ordered, "you stay right where you are."

Ernie looked at Nina. Her eyes were wide with fright

and one hand covered her partially open mouth as if she were forcing back a cry. Ernie realized the fire was heading in the direction of the Lacours' place. He went over to Nina and touched her shoulder. "Don't be scared," he said. "We'll get your mom and the kids out of there." He saw his sisters and his father staring at him. He went beet red.

"Ernie," his father broke the silence, "we'd better get going."

Outside the orange and yellow sky looked like a child's crayon drawing of a sunset. "We'll see if we can hitch a ride with Mr. Bacon," Dr. Hemingway said. They headed for Bacons' farm but they hadn't gotten halfway before they heard a wagon coming toward them. Mr. Bacon reined in the horses. Dr. Hemingway and Ernie climbed up beside him. Mr. Bacon was breathing hard. "Must've got this rig together in two minutes flat. Sheriff come by and told me. I'm not sure but what I've got my pants on backwards. Couldn't have happened at a worse time. Grass is like tinder. I wish I knew how to coax that rain out of the sky."

"How do you think the fire got started?" Ernie asked Mr. Bacon.

"Hard to say. I suppose some fool dropped a match. Or it could've been a chimney fire. Two or three shacks back in there. Mostly Indians. They have to make do with those makeshift stoves."

"The woods around there are covered with slashings," Dr. Hemingway said. Ernie had hiked through that area and knew what his father meant. When the land was timbered the loggers had left the branches and the tops of the pine trees. The slashings were piled up higher than your head and so dry that any spark could set them off.

When they reached the Lacours', they saw Mrs. Lacour up on the roof. Nina's younger sister, Sue, who wasn't more than six or seven, was staggering under the weight of hauling a pail of water from the well. She handed it to her brother, Billy, who was a year or two older. Billy dragged the pail, splashing and spilling, up the ladder to his mother. Their sad-looking horse and wagon were hitched to a tree. The wagon had been loaded with a trunk and some bits of furniture.

Mr. Bacon pulled up the horses. "Mrs. Lacour," he shouted, "you get those kids and get out of here."

Mrs. Lacour had long black hair like Nina's. Usually it was fastened around her head in a braid. Now her hair hung over her face. Her dress was soaking wet and clung to her body. She was a large woman and standing up there on top of the roof with the dark sky behind her, she looked, Ernie thought, like some sort of Amazon ready to fight off the fire single-handedly. "I don't go," she called to them. "Pete, he say to stay here and wet down the roof. Him and Ted, they coming back for us. Him and Ted they hunt a little. He say in a fire all the animals run out of the woods right into your gun."

Mr. Bacons shouted up at her, "You're crazy. That fire's getting closer." But she wouldn't come down.

Mr. Bacon snapped the reins and hurried the horses

by. "The Kleins' farm is up ahead. We'll tell them to stop by for her." His voice was rough. He didn't like leaving Mrs. Lacour.

But when they got to the Kleins' farm they found it deserted. The front door was swinging open as though whoever had walked out last had not been optimistic enough to close it. "Too late to go back," Bacon said. "They'll be needing us up ahead. She'll leave when the fire starts edging up. Their horse and wagon were all set to go."

Ernie saw two hares streaking through the grass. He tried not to think of the porcupines and groundhogs who moved slowly or the hollow trees and burrows where families of squirrels and mice, too small to escape, would be trapped. The idea of Nina's father shooting down the escaping animals made him sick.

Rounding a curve they came to a field crowded with wagons. There were even a few automobiles. At the end of the field was a hill. At the top of the hill, silhouetted against the glow of the flames, a crew of fifty or more men were desperately digging a trench. Heavy smoke gave the sky the unnatural darkness of a violent thunderstorm or an eclipse of the sun. Bent over, swinging their shovels in the eerie shadows, the men looked to Ernie like trolls laboring below the ground on some sinister task.

"They found themselves quite a crew," Bacon said. When a forest fire threatened, the sheriff could come along and draft any able-bodied man he needed.

"What are they doing?" Ernie asked.

"They're making a control line," his father said. "They dig a wide trench to clear the soil of brush or grass or anything that might burn and hope that when the fire gets there, it will stop because there won't be anything to feed it. It's at the top of the hill so the drafts coming up from this side will work against the fire." He turned to Bacon, "It doesn't look to me as if its going to hold. What do you think?"

"I got my doubts. The fire's not more than two, three miles from here and moving fast."

"Well, we'd better do what we can," Dr. Hemingway said.

They tied up the wagon and headed for the crest of the hill. Gusts of hot wind blew over them. Most of the men had stripped to their undershirts. Their clothes lay on the ground in small heaps of color like exotic plants springing up from the earth. As Ernie and the two men peeled off their shirts, Jim Nordstrom, one of the sheriff's deputies, stopped shoveling and came over. "Sure can use your help with this firebreak. If it gets over the hill it'll spread to the houses and farms down the road." Ernie wondered if Mrs. Lacour had left by now.

Before he could finish taking off his shirt, his father had started shoveling. When Ernie dug his own shovel into the ground, he found the sod fastened to the earth with thick tangles of grass and the woody roots of trees. He pushed the shovel in hard with his foot and broke though the roots. Sweat rolled down his face. After the sod was cleared he was into sandy soil and the work went faster. In the background the fire roared like wind down a chimney, only a hundred times louder.

Ernie could see his father just ahead of him, his shovel swinging rhythmically as it bit into the ground and flung away the sand in one easy movement. Ernie tried to match his dad's pace but it was too fast for him. He was surprised to see how muscular his father's back was.

The leaves on the trees seemed to be withering and dying before their eyes. A man came by with a water pail and dipper. Ernie could have drunk the whole bucket but he tried not to take more than his share. He didn't know how much longer he could keep shoveling. Breathing was nearly impossible. Some of the men had wet their handkerchiefs and tied them over their noses.

The fire grew louder. It sounded like cannons being shot off. Firebrands were falling all around them, igniting the dry grass. The men tried to put the sparks out with a shovelful of sand but it was becoming impossible to keep up.

Dr. Hemingway looked around at Ernie. "Maybe you'd better go back to the wagon and rest up a little."

Ernie shook his head and made himself shovel faster. Tears were running down his face from the sting of the smoke. He could feel the raw bite of broken blisters on his hands. Suddenly the man in front of his father dropped to the ground. Dr. Hemingway hurried over. He put an ear to the man's chest and listened. "Just a touch of heatstroke," he said to Jim Nordstrom. "Better get him out of here." He motioned Ernie to help.

"You take the feet, son," Jim Nordstrom said. "It's Casper Slip. I know this dirty old geezer. Doesn't wash from one year to the next. Don't want to be anywhere near those feet." They half-carried, half-dragged the man, whose eyes were open now and wandering around in their sockets like they had come loose. Casper was heavy but Ernie was glad to be relieved of the shoveling. Probably his dad had picked him to help on purpose. They heaved Slip onto one of the wagons. Nordstrom got a pail of water and splashed it over him. He jerked into a sitting position, cursing and spitting water. "No point complaining," Nordstrom said. "You needed that bath, Casper."

When they turned back to the hill they found the men had stopped shoveling and were staring at the little balls of fire that exploded over their heads like shooting stars. The wind was carrying the sparks beyond the trench and down the near side of the hill. Ernie could see that in no time they would be cut off.

"We're losing ground," Nordstrom shouted over the fire's roar. "We got to get our wagons out of here. That fire's traveling near as fast as we can. We'll cut across the field over to the pike and build a backfire there."

"What about those Indian shacks?" a man called.

Nordstrom shook his head. "Can't be helped. We got to stop the fire."

"Dad." Ernie's voice was urgent. "We've got to go

back and see if the Lacours have gotten out of there. I promised Nina I'd see they were all right.

Dr. Hemingway gave Ernie a long look. "Bacon," he said, "you and Ernie go with the others. I'd like to borrow your rig and see if I can get to the Lacours'."

"You're welcome to my wagon, Doc, but I don't know if you can make it," Mr. Bacon said. "That fire's moving awful fast. Maybe I'd better go along."

"Thanks, but they need all the hands they can get to fight the fire."

"I want to go with you," Ernie said.

"No, Ernie. You go with Mr. Bacon. That's an order." His father's face was smudged with dirt. The black beard and dark eyes with their heavy black brows gave his face a formidable look. Ernie obeyed.

The wagons were pulling away. Ernie climbed into the back of Nordstrom's rig while Mr. Bacon got up onto the driver's seat next to Nordstrom. The smoke roiled up into the sky. It was dark as night and nearly impossible to breathe. Bacon and Nordstrom were shouting to one another over the noise of the fire, paying no attention to Ernie. All at once Ernie was scrambling down into the darkness and running across to where his father was hitching the wagon. Moving carefully so his father wouldn't see him, he waited until the horses started and then caught at the back of the wagon, hoisting himself up. He sat there trying to figure out how the man driving the wagon could be the same man he had seen earlier that day in the kitchen at Windemere messing around with pots and pans.

A flaming branch landed in the back of the wagon. Ernie kicked it off. He felt better about disobeying his father. If he hadn't been there the wagon might have burned. He inched his way up to the driver's seat and touched his father's shoulder. His father twisted around.

"Dammit, Ernie. I told you not to come."

Ernie had never heard his father swear before. Dr. Hemingway looked in the direction of the receding wagons. They were well out of sight. He motioned Ernie up onto the seat next to him. But Ernie pointed to the scorched place on the wagon, signaling that he ought to keep an eye out for other sparks. His father nodded.

It was frightening to think that they were all alone and the rest of the men were heading in the other direction. Sparks flew through the air like small red birds and lighted onto the fields. Wherever they fell, flames shot up and there was no one to put them out. Fire was racing along the field to the left of them. The wagon itself was hot to the touch. As quickly as sparks fell on the wagon, Ernie ground them out. He prayed that one wouldn't land on him or his father. A white jagged light cut through the darkened sky. Lightning. If only the rain would come. He concentrated on trying to pull it out of the sky. When they came to the Kleins' farm there was nothing left but two heaps of smoldering timbers that had once been a house and a barn. Dr. Hemingway hurried the horses on.

In the smoke and darkness you could barely see the road. The horses were skittish and panting from the heat. They had nearly reached the Lacours' when the fire swept in front of them, crossing the road and sending up a barricade of flames. Dr. Hemingway shouted to Ernie to hang on and urged the horses forward but they were terrified by the flames and panicked, galloping out of control. Ernie hung onto the sides of the wagon to keep from being thrown out. The fire had sprung up directly in front of them. There was no getting through.

All at once there was a wind that wasn't the wind of the fire and a second darkness that wasn't the darkness of smoke and a rumbling sound that wasn't the fire's roar. Rain poured down on them. Ernie turned his face up and opened his mouth. The rain pelted him, forcing his eyes shut. The horses, surprised into obedience by the downpour, responded meekly to Dr. Hemingway as he turned the wagon around toward the fire and brought it to a halt.

Ernie climbed up next to his father. "What about the Lacours?" he asked almost afraid to say the words.

Dr. Hemingway shook his head. "I'm afraid the fire got there before the rain. We'll know in a minute as soon as the fire dies down enough so we can make it through the woods."

They were both silent. Rain poured down on them. The wagon was filling with water. The horses bent down and eagerly licked at a puddle. The flames disappeared in one spot and leapt up in another. The fields were white with steaming smoke. The whole forest gave off the smell of a thousand doused campfires. The doctor snapped the reins and urged the horses back toward the road.

Ernie wished he were somewhere else. He didn't want

to face what might be waiting for them at the Lacours'. He had to tell his father. He couldn't keep it back any longer. "Dad, you've got to take Nina back to Oak Park with us. I told her if you wouldn't I'd marry her."

He thought his father would be furious but all he said was, "Don't you think you're a little young for that, Ernie?"

"She's got to get away from home. Her dad's after them all the time."

"I don't know that two children like you getting married would be the solution."

Ernie had no time to resent being called a child. The fire was out and his dad was guiding the wagon along the road toward the Lacours'.

From a distance it appeared that the house was still standing, but as they drew closer they found the roof was gone, leaving only a few charred partitions. Tags of wallpaper hung down in scorched shreds from the walls. The shed behind the house where they kept the horse had burned to the ground. For a moment they thought the Lacours had escaped. Then they saw the remains of the wagon and the horse's burned flesh. The horse was still tethered to the tree. Ernie looked away.

"You wait here, son," Dr. Hemingway said. His voice had a searching anger as though he were looking for someone to blame.

Ernie couldn't have moved if he had wanted to. He had been ready enough to follow his father into the danger and excitement of the fire. All the excitement was gone now. Ernie thought that sometimes it was terrible to have the kind of imagination he had. He could picture things too vividly. They appeared before his eyes when he didn't want them there.

A sound, something like the mewing of a cat, reached him through the splatter of the rain. It came again and this time it sounded like a child's cry. A second later he heard a muffled call. The sounds had a hollow ringing echo. His father heard them, too. Together they ran across the slippery burned-over ground to the well. They reached it at the same time. Peering down into the darkness they could hear Mrs. Lacour sobbing for help and the children whimpering. Inside the rim of the well Ernie could feel an iron ladder. He eased himself down rung by rung. Mrs. Lacour was climbing up toward him, urging the children ahead of her. "He never come back," she kept saying. "I tell him I wait. But he never come." When Ernie got hold of Nina's sister Sue, she clung to him so hard she nearly pulled him off the ladder. He could feel her trembling against his chest. He handed her up to his father.

"You're going to be all right," Dr. Hemingway reassured her. "We'll have you safe and dry in no time."

Billy climbed silently up to Ernie and let himself be boosted over the well's edge, where he clung to Dr. Hemingway as if he were the only thing floating on a wide ocean.

Ernie reached down for Mrs. Lacour's hand and felt the firmness of her grip with relief. She followed him out, caught up the two children, and held them to her.

Her skirts were dripping water. "We saw fire coming," the words rushed out. "We saw it coming right at us and I made the children go into the well. They didn't want to 'cause I always warn them not to lean over or they fall in and drown and they afraid. But the fire, it just kept coming and he never come back and it was so hot the shed burn so I finally got them down. Then fire rushed over the well. We seen its reflection in the water below us— just like a round mirror. It looked so funny. I don't know how long we hung onto the ladder. I was scared the kids would let go and fall in the water. Then I felt rain but I couldn't get the children to follow me up. They thought the fire was still there. Then we hear your voices. You tell him it wasn't my fault . . ."

They got her in the wagon and handed up the children. She was still muttering, "They never come back. They never come back." Over and over. All the way to Windemere she kept telling the story. At first the children listened open-mouthed and silent to the story of their narrow escape, but after a while they prompted her if she left any parts out and even added some things of their own.

It was ten in the evening and the rain had stopped. Ernie and Dr. Hemingway were sitting on the front porch. Nina and Mrs. Lacour were helping the girls put together some clothes for the children to wear.

Mrs. Hemingway was trying to soothe Billy and Sue into sleep. Ernie could hear his mother's deep rich voice singing some child's song he hadn't heard in years. It sounded light and pleasant and could nearly make you forget what had happened that day.

In spite of all the rain the acrid smell of smoke still hung in the air. "Well," Dr. Hemingway said, "I'll have to get the pickles finished tomorrow." He sounded as though he had been interrupted that day by nothing more than a casual visitor lingering over a cup of coffee. "Son, I want you to know that even though you disobeyed me, I was proud to have you with me today."

Ernie flushed. He didn't know how his father could come right out and say something so personal. Even if his father messed around in the kitchen, he loved him more than anyone else in the world. But he couldn't tell him that.

His father hadn't mentioned Nina. Ernie supposed he would give him a lecture when things calmed down. He didn't care what his father said. As much as he loved his dad, he loved Nina more. He would marry her and take care of her. She didn't even have a home to go to anymore. After supper he had seen his dad talking to his mother. Ernie was sure he was telling her all about him and Nina. Tomorrow he'd probably catch hell. It wouldn't bother him any. He remembered the way Nina had looked at him when he and his dad had walked into the cottage with Mrs. Lacour and the kids. He'd never give Nina up.

10

Nina Goes Away

In the morning when Ernie awoke the fire seemed like a dream. It was like a chapter in a book he had read or a story someone had told him. The danger and the excitement were still there but it seemed to have happened to someone else—until he looked out of his bedroom window. The sun was up, but it shone through a smoky haze. Sunlight lay above the land sandwiched between layers of smoke. The air that came in his window smelled like a kitchen where someone had burned the toast. The fire had been real.

He hurried into his clothes. This was the day he would have to convince his dad that Nina ought to go back with them to Oak Park. His father knew now about his promise to Nina. Ernie was sure he wouldn't refuse. If he did, Ernie would have to find a way to take care of Nina.

He had slept later than usual. His father and sisters already had eaten their breakfast. Dr. Hemingway had made pancakes for everyone. Mrs. Hemingway was having a tray in her room. Billy and Sue and Sunny were still at the table. Nina and Mrs. Lacour were in their room.

"Why was Nina crying?" Ernie heard Billy ask.

Dr. Hemingway saw the look of alarm on Ernie's face. "It's nothing to worry about, Billy. Your sister is still upset about yesterday. Ernie, how about some griddle cakes?"

Ernie decided Nina was worried about the fire and the damage it had done to their home. He thought it was sort of indecent to have a big breakfast when Nina had been crying, but his dad's buckwheat pancakes were a special treat, offered only once or twice a summer. "Just a few," he said. He hoped his father wouldn't take him too seriously, because he was plenty hungry.

A big stack of cakes appeared in front of him. Dr. Hemingway had made pancakes with ears and tails for Billy and Sue. "How about a second helping of rabbits?" he asked them.

"Ernie only wanted a *few,*" Sunny said. "I could eat the rest."

Ernie pulled his plate closer and reached for some of his dad's strawberry jam. "You already had your breakfast."

"I'll make you some more, Sunny. Ernie, as soon as you finish up, I want you to go over to Horton Bay and reimburse Jim Dilworth for the fine he paid for you."

"I've been giving him a few trout," Ernie said cautiously.

"That's nice of you, Ernie. But I'm sure you weren't

giving them in exchange for the money he lent you. *That* would be the same as selling them and *that's* illegal. There's enough poaching going on here without my son getting involved in it. You can pay me back this winter from your snow shoveling jobs."

The thought of the small sums he made each winter shoveling snow was sobering. Certainly he couldn't support Nina on that kind of money. When he returned from the Dilworths' he'd *have* to find a way to get his parents to take Nina home. He hoped his dad would agree now that he knew how he felt about her.

The trip to Horton Bay took longer than he had planned. Uncle Jim had wanted to hear all about the fire and made him tell the story of Mrs. Lacour and the children hiding out in the well, twice.

"The Lord was surely with them," Aunty Beth said. She made Ernie eat a huge lunch of deviled eggs and cold pork chops and blackberry pie. "After an experience like that, you must be starved." Aunty Beth believed there wasn't anything so bad that food couldn't make better.

All the way back Ernie thought about Nina. She could live with them while Ernie finished high school. He'd get all the jobs he could and save his money so they could get married as soon as possible. What did he care if he didn't go to college? He didn't want to be a doctor anyhow. All that blood and stuff. He'd start writing as soon as he got back to Oak Park. Nina could tell him all her Indian stories. When he got out of school he'd get a job with the Oak Park paper. He thought of how surprised his friends at school would be when they found out he had a girl friend. More than just a girl friend, a fiancée. When they saw Nina's long black hair and found out she was a real Indian, or at least half one, they'd be green with envy.

His dad was standing at the end of the dock waiting for him. That wasn't like his dad, Ernie thought. His dad didn't stand around and wait for people. He considered that a waste of time.

"Well, Ernie, you took a little longer than I expected."

"Aunty Beth wanted me to stay for lunch."

"I'm sure that was a treat. I thought we might do some fishing this afternoon. Maybe wade the little creek on that spit of beach over at Longfield."

"Sure." Ernie was pleased. His dad was going fishing with him instead of fussing around the kitchen, stuffing everything that grew into glass jars.

They toured the garden and orchard at Longfield first. "You've done a fine job over here, Ernie. The fruit trees never looked better."

Ernie was puzzled. First, his father standing at the dock, then the fishing trip in the middle of the afternoon and now all this praise. It wasn't like his dad. He began to feel uneasy.

When they reached the creek they found the bank crisscrossed with deer tracks. His father studied the prints of the hooves. "Look at this one, Ernie. See how deep it goes. Plenty of weight on that one. A big buck, most likely."

"Maybe we could come back this fall during the deer season," Ernie said. "We could hunt the old buck. Nina could come with us. It would give her a chance to visit her mom and Ted and the kids."

Dr. Hemingway gave Ernie a quick look but didn't answer him. Ernie was encouraged. His dad wasn't saying they *couldn't* come or that Nina might *not* be with them in Oak Park. He wouldn't push his dad about that right now. He'd talk to him after supper. Anyhow, the creek was no place to talk. It was narrow, not more than four feet wide. You waded though a dense tunnel of overhanging shrubs and trees. Any noise spooked the trout and a careless cast decorated the brush with a tangle of fishing line. Dr. Hemingway let Ernie go ahead, giving him the first chance at the trout.

Between them they pulled in just under a dozen small brookies. They were the prettiest fish you could catch, Ernie thought. The speckles of pink and salmon and lavender on their sides formed fractured rainbows. "We'll have enough for dinner." Ernie said, pleased to be bringing in a good catch for Nina to see.

His dad was busy gutting the fish and didn't answer. But on the way back across the lake Dr. Hemingway began to talk about his brother who was a missionary doctor in China. "I've never said much to you, Ernie, but I think a lot about your Uncle Will. He's seen the world and I'm stuck in Oak Park. I used to have dreams about being a medical missionary myself. Going to some place like Guam or Greenland. But once you're married you start having a family and you're tied down for life. The time to see the world is when you're young, Ernie. You've got all the time in the world for marrying and having a family." His father looked at him out of the corner of his eye.

Ernie didn't like the way the conversation was going. His father added hastily, "I wouldn't want you to get the idea that I don't love your mother and you and your sisters and brother. I thank God for our fine family. It's only that I wonder sometimes what the rest of the world is like. I wonder what *other* lives I might have had."

Ernie knew what his father was saying, but he knew he couldn't give Nina up. Right now all he was thinking of was getting back to Windemere and seeing her.

When they did get back Ernie found there were only enough places at the table for his parents and sisters and himself. "Aren't the Lacours eating with us?" He was afraid someone had taken sick.

No one said anything for a minute. His mother was reaching in the cupboard for their dinner plates. His dad was melting bacon grease in the frying pan for the trout. Marce was dropping ears of corn into boiling water. Sunny was the only other one in the kitchen. "Didn't you know, Ernie? They all went away this morning."

Ernie couldn't believe his ears. "What do you mean, 'went away'? *Who* went away?"

Mr. Lacour and Ted came and took Nina and her mom and Billy and Sue away with them."

"Where did they go?" Ernie thought maybe they were staying at the Bacon farm where there was more room.

"They're going to stay with some friends over at the Indian camp," his mother explained.

"Nina isn't," Sunny said.

"Where's Nina staying?" Ernie asked. Things were moving too fast for him.

"The fact is, Ernie," his father said, "Your mother and I were both impressed with what a nice girl Nina is. How bright she is. We thought she ought to have a better chance for schooling than she's getting here. And we thought about how you said she wasn't happy at home."

"You mean she's coming back with us to Oak Park?" Nothing else made sense but Ernie felt that wasn't the way it was going to be. His mouth was so dry he could hardly force his lips apart to ask the question.

"Your mother and I didn't think that would be practical. We've been very fortunate to make arrangements for Nina to board at the Indian school in Harbor Springs this fall. In the meantime she'll stay with an aunt and uncle in Petoskey. Her uncle came down this morning and got her."

"That's why you sent me to Horton Bay!"

"Ernest, you must believe we thought it was the best thing for both of you." His father looked worried.

"You never even let me say goodbye to her!"

"We didn't want any scenes, Ernie. We thought the less fuss the better," his mother soothed.

"Nina didn't want to go," Sunny said.

"Sunny, you keep out of this." Mrs. Hemingway tried to put an arm around Ernie's shoulder, but he pulled away and ran to his room. Since his father's return he had been sleeping at Windemere instead of his camp at Longfield. He slammed his door behind him and flung himself face down on his bed. What could he do? He could go after Nina, only he didn't know just where in Petoskey she might be. He would have to go from door to door. Maybe he should just run away. He'd hitchhike up to Canada and join the Canadian army. Whatever he did, he wouldn't spend another night at Windemere. He folded up a change of clothes in his blanket. At the last minute he decided to take his shotgun in case he had to hunt his own food. He left a note for Sunny asking her to take his library books back to Oak Park and telling her she could have his tent. His fly rod was to go to Ted Lacour. Writing the note made him feel awful. As if he were dead or something. He wondered what a war was like. People got wounded and killed in a war. He imagined how his mother and dad would feel learning he had been injured on the field of battle and knowing it was their fault.

Someone knocked at his door. He mumbled, "Let me alone." When the knocking stopped he made a mound in his bed with a pillow and covered it over with a blanket. He waited until it was dark and then he climbed carefully out of his window and edged toward the boat. It was the end of August and darkness came early now. They'd think he was asleep. They wouldn't come looking to see if the boat were there.

He always prided himself on how quietly he could maneuver the boat across the lake. As quietly as any Indian paddling a canoe. He kept close to the shoreline so the boat would meld with the shadows of the trees along the bank. He'd spend one last night at Longfield. In the morning he'd take off before sunrise. Somehow he'd find Nina in Petoskey and say goodbye to her; then he'd leave for Canada and the war.

Longfield was just ahead. It had been a couple of weeks since he had broken camp. He was looking forward to sleeping out again. He had missed the reassuring ripple of the spring and the creak of the hemlock trees. How complicated his life had become since he first camped out in June. He'd probably never have another chance to spend the night at Longfield.

He was feeling plenty sorry for himself when he noticed a flashlight down on the spit. At first he thought his family had found out where he had gone and somehow had gotten there before him. But that wasn't possible. He moved the boat forward silently, hardly touching the oars to the water. The light disappeared. The next minute he heard the crack of rifles, two or three of them. Poachers. He was sure of it. They were shining the deer and when the deer, attracted by the flashlight, moved in, they shot them. For a moment all he could think of was getting out of there fast before they saw him. But then he had another thought. He had his shotgun. Suppose he sneaked up on the poachers and caught them all single-handedly. Maybe there would be a reward. Enough so he could find Nina and marry her. Anyhow he'd get his name in the paper for sure and she'd see it. And his dad would know he wasn't just a kid. For the first time since he had heard that Nina had been sent away, he began to feel hopeful.

Ernie made himself move cautiously, letting the boat drift in toward the shore a few hundred feet above the spit. In the dark no one could see him. He beached the boat, reached for his gun and loaded it. Instead of going along the open shore, he crept up to the little stream where he and his dad had fished that morning and began following it down to where it emptied out at the spit. There was plenty of cover and he knew every inch of the bank.

When he was almost at the spit, he stopped. The men were whispering excitedly to one another but he couldn't make out their words. He wasn't sure exactly what he should say. "Stick 'em up" sounded more like he was in the wrong. He decided on, "Drop your guns."

Something else began to bother him. How would he get them back across the lake? He supposed he would have to keep them there all night until his parents were up and looking for him. Then he could hoist his shirt as a signal. Sunny would be sure to see it.

The more he tried to figure things out the more he began to wish he were in his own bedroom at Windemere. It occurred to him that it would not be too late to turn back. He could still get to his boat without the poachers knowing he had been there. Then he could row home and tell his dad to get the game warden, Tommy Thrake's father. But thinking of Tommy kept him where he was. He could see Tommy's face fall when he heard Ernie Hemingway had caught the poachers Tommy and his father had been after for months. And caught them single-handedly. He'd be even with Tommy for squealing on him about the blue heron.

Suddenly he realized the voices had stopped. Everything was dark and quiet. Had they gone? Maybe he had lost his big chance. He didn't know whether he was glad or sorry. A hand grabbed his collar and yanked him up. Another hand wrestled his gun away. Someone had their arm around his neck and was dragging him down to the spit. They had such a tight grip around his throat that he couldn't even scream. The beam of a flashlight stabbed his face.

"Damn! Doc Hemingway's boy!" The voice was Mr. Lacour's.

11

Poachers

Mr. Lacour let Ernie go. Ernie gave Nina's dad what he hoped was a friendly, devil-may-care grin, as though it was the middle of the afternoon and Ernie had just been strolling along the beach minding his own business. "Hello there, Mr. Lacour," he managed to get out.

Mr. Lacour was a big-shouldered, hefty man with black curly hair and a black curled beard. Ernie had always thought all he needed was a single earring and a parrot on his shoulder to pass for a pirate. "Shut up, Ernie," he growled. When he was angry his French-Canadian accent was more noticeable. "I told you to keep away from here."

"I just thought I'd do a little night fishing," Ernie said. In the darkness he couldn't make out the faces of the other men but he knew they would not believe him. He had been carrying a shotgun, not a fishing pole. They were shining the flashlight into his face so he couldn't see them. But in the minute when they had wrestled him out of the bushes he had recognized the other two men as Sam, an Indian who did odd jobs for the summer people, and a white man, Dan Groff. Groff had been kicked out of his job at the sawmill across the lake. There was talk he had gotten into a fight with the superintendent and nearly killed him.

Ernie had seen something else. Three deer lying there in a pool of blood. A couple of does and a buck with a big rack. Probably the one who made those deep prints his father had noticed. He remembered what a pleasant place the little stream had seemed in the early afternoon with the sun working its way through the thick tangle of green brush and lighting the surface of the water so that you could see right down to the gold sand on the stream's bed. Now it was all different. The trees and brush were ominous dark shapes, the stream a snakelike black ribbon.

"We better tie him up," Mr. Lacour said. "Then we get our deer in the boat and get out fast. They won't find him till morning."

"You're crazy," Groff said. "He saw our faces. The minute he gets loose they'll be out looking for us. You know what kind'a jail sentence we'll pull? They got a good idea how much venison we send downstate. They'll lock us up five years for sure. I've done all the time I'm gonna do."

"Maybe he'll keep his mouth shut." Sam said.

"Him?" Groff laughed. "He's got one of the biggest mouths around here."

"So what do we do?" Mr. Lacour said.

"He must've come in a boat." Groff prodded Ernie with the butt of his rifle. It was meant to hurt and it did. "You got a boat?"

"I beached it just down the shore. In that grove of birch." Ernie was trying to be cooperative but he was so frightened he could hardly talk. His only hope was that they would just take his boat away so they could escape before he got back to Windemere.

"Go and get it," Groff said to Sam.

"What you got in mind?" Mr. Lacour asked. His voice was casual and interested.

Ernie listened for the answer. He had begun to realize his life might depend on it.

"What we're going to do," Groff said, pride in his voice as though he had solved some hopelessly complicated puzzle, "is set him adrift in the boat."

Sam was back wading in the water, the boat riding along behind him. "We keep the oars, eh?" he said.

"No, we *don't* keep the oars. We give *him* the oars." Groff sounded pleased at how he was thinking faster then they were.

Ernie felt his heart racing. Groff was enjoying himself too much.

"Just tell us your plan," Mr. Lacour said. "We got no time for games."

"We cut a hole in the boat and then we hit him over the head and tow him out into the lake. It looks like he rammed into something in the dark and rowed out before he knew about the leak. They'll think his drowning is an accident."

Ernie's body was drenched with sweat. The breeze off the lake blew over him, evaporating the moisture and chilling him to the bone. He was trying to keep from shivering so they wouldn't see how afraid he was, but he was sure they could hear his teeth chatter. He wondered what would happen if he just started running, but Groff was holding a rifle on him and Groff had just suggested killing him.

Lacour said in a matter of fact voice, "No good. I don't get mixed up in that."

Ernie was relieved Mr. Lacour was against the idea, but how could he sound so calm talking about the awful thing Groff wanted to do to him?

"You don't have to. Sam and me'll do it. You got no guts, Lacour. We got a good thing going. I ain't letting no kid cheat me out of my money. Sam and me can divide the profits. We don't need you. The sooner you get going the better." For a second Groff pointed the rifle threateningly at Mr. Lacour. But before Ernie could even think of taking off, the rifle was back aimed at this chest.

"What's the matter with you, Groff?" Mr. Lacour said. "What do I care for him? His family come and buy up land so there's no place to hunt anymore. All the time they're messing in my family's business. Get rid of him. Come on. Sooner the better. You and Sam dress out the deer. I'll take care of the kid." He wrapped his arm around

Ernie's neck and began to pull him toward the boat.

Ernie tried to struggle but Mr. Lacour's grip was like a steel band.

Groff pointed the rifle at Ernie's head. Ernie stopped struggling. Groff ordered Sam, "Take your knife and put a hole in that boat. Not too big. We don't want it to sink until we get it away from here. Then come back and give me a hand with the deer."

Sam moved down to the boat. Ernie saw the glitter of the knife in his hand. The hand went up and down sawing at the boat. Ernie winced at the scraping noise. For a minute all he could think of was trying to explain the damage to his father. Then he realized he wouldn't be there to explain it. He started to say something to Mr. Lacour, to plead with him. But the minute he opened his mouth Mr. Lacour told him roughly to shut up and tightened his grip.

Sam looked at Lacour and hurried back to Groff, who was dressing out the deer, thankful to be leaving Lacour and Ernie and what was going to happen next.

Lacour pulled Ernie down toward the boat and pushed him in. He had dropped the flashlight so he could use both hands. Ernie tried to squeeze away but Mr. Lacour had his hands around Ernie's throat. "You groan," he whispered. "You groan good and loud when I tell you. I ain't forget you save my Nina that night and what your dad did in the fire for my wife and kids. But remember keep your mouth shut about what you see tonight or I come after you." He had a boulder in his hand. Ernie stopped breathing. Mr. Lacour raised the boulder and brought it down on a life jacket. It made a sickening noise. "Now!" Mr. Lacour hissed.

Ernie let out a loud moan.

"Good. No more noise now." Mr. Lacour brought the boulder down a second time. "You keep away from my Nina," he whispered. "Keep still. You'll be all right." Mr. Lacour went to help Sam and Groff load the deer onto their launch.

Ernie lay there terrified, waiting as long as he could between breaths. He was afraid they might somehow hear him breathing.

"That's six deer we're sending down this week," Groff was saying. "With the ducks and partridge that'll be a couple of hundred for us. And you were going to let that big mouth go. You sure you put him to sleep good?"

"He's not gonna make any trouble," Mr. Lacour said. "I'll get a tow rope on his boat. You get the motor goin' and let's get out of here."

The motor on their launch started up and Ernie felt a jerk as his boat followed after it. The water was seeping in slowly through the slash. The boat might sink before they cut him loose. Or they might tow him out so far he couldn't swim to shore. Suddenly the boat stopped its rapid movement and was bobbing lightly on the surface of the water.

Ernie wanted to climb out and start swimming, but

he knew he would have to force himself to wait until their boat was well away. Sounds carried over the lake. It was good he waited because a minute later the beam of their flashlight swept over him as he lay motionless on the bottom of the boat.

There was more water coming in now. He had to lie there and let it gradually inch up over his body. He made himself wait until he could no longer hear the motor of the launch. His boat was filling up fast. He sat up and tried to see the shore, but the lake was a circle of darkness. The shore might be anywhere. He slipped over the side of the boat and swam around its edge until he found the severed tow rope. He was afraid of drowning and he was afraid of the poachers, but more than anything he was afraid of what his father would say if something happened to the boat. He'd never be able to explain it without giving Mr. Lacour away and he couldn't do that. Mr. Lacour had saved his life. If he told his father what he knew, his father would tell Thrake and then they'd put Mr. Lacour in jail and he, Ernie, would be responsible. What would Nina think of him then?

He pulled on a rope attached to the prow. The weight of the water-filled boat was going to keep him from making any distance. In the darkness he might just swim in a circle until he sank from exhaustion. He would have to let go and dive down to the lake bottom to see how deep the lake was here and what the bottom was like. He had fished the lake so many years that knowing those things might help him guess what part of the lake he was in.

He dropped the tow line and dove. Like a slap in the face, the firm sandy floor of the lake came at him. He couldn't believe it. He was on a sand bar. He stood up. The water only reached his shoulders. When he slid into the water he had assumed it was in a deep part of the lake. It had never occurred to him to simply stand up. Hadn't they wanted him to drown? He realized Mr. Lacour, who knew just about every inch of the lake, had been careful to cut the boat loose when they were over the sand bar, counting on Groff and Sam's ignorance of the lake bottom.

He nearly let out a yelp of joy. Reaching for the boat, he tipped it and got most of the water out. Hanging on to the tow rope, he began wading toward shore. There was a drop-off where he had to swim, but the boat was lighter now and he knew where he was going.

Once he reached the shore, he began walking along in the shallow water toward Windemere. From time to time he had to stop to empty the boat or to maneuver it around old docks or deadheads. When he got too cold, he'd plunge into the lake and swim a few strokes, escaping from the cold air that rode over the top of the water. He lost any sense of time. He wasn't sure whether he had been in the lake an hour or several hours when he heard the distant sound of a motor. He stumbled up onto the shore and hid the boat in among the alder bushes, crouching down beside it. The motor grew louder. A flashlight swept back and forth across the lake and then switched off. In a few minutes there was silence again over the water. Ernie started breathing again.

It took him a long time to get the boat back into the water. He had never been so tired in his life. He knew when he started out that he had been a couple of miles from Windemere. Now there was a thin line of light along the eastern horizon. He made himself hurry. He would have to put the boat in the boat house. They were leaving the next day for Oak Park. He'd tell his dad he had awakened early and put it in for winter storage. By next summer when the damage was discovered, no one would know how or when it had happened.

He was startled to realize that when he thought of the family making the trip back to Oak Park, he thought of himself as going along. There was no point now in running away. He couldn't see Nina, at least for a long time. He owed that to Mr. Lacour. Anyhow, he didn't want to make Mr. Lacour angry. He wished he could tell someone about what had happened. It would make a great story for his school magazine. He'd have to disguise the names. And he'd see that at least in the story Groff got what he deserved. He knew he could write it.

The thin line along the horizon widened to a band of the palest orange. Ahead of him was Windemere. Everyone was asleep. His mother, his father, his sisters, none of them had any idea of what had happened to him. If he ever told them the story they'd think it was all his imagination. That he had made it up.

Later that morning when he woke up in the safety of his own bed, sunlight everywhere, the smell of his dad's homemade pork sausage frying, the sounds of his mother crooning to Leicester and Sunny calling out to him to come for a last swim, he thought perhaps he had.

Afterword

Ernest Hemingway returned to the Hemingway home in Oak Park. During his next two years of high school he wrote many short stories for his high school publication, the *Trapeze*. He graduated from high school in 1917. After a summer at Windemere, Ernest began work as a reporter for the *Kansas City Star*. In April 1918 he left the *Star,* and after a final fishing trip to Horton Bay he enlisted in the American Field Service as an ambulance driver. On May 23 he sailed on the *Chicago* for Europe and World War I.

Acknowledgments

While I have written fiction and not a biography, I have tried to present the author as he might have been as a boy. I am indebted to the following sources for suggesting incidents and providing background. The story of the barn dance and the game of "Truth" were suggested by Madelaine Hemingway Miller's autobiograhical book, *Ernie*. The story of the blue heron appears in all the books dealing with Hemingway's youth, and Hemingway himself wrote a story, "The Last Good Country," about it. Ernie's friendship with Nina is based on several local stories and Hemingway's own boasts, but the extent of the friendship has never been confirmed.

I would especially to like to thank Ernest Hemingway Mainland, Ernest Hemingway's nephew, for making several helpful corrections to the original manuscript. After the death of his mother, Madelaine (Sunny) Hemingway Miller, Mr. Mainland inherited Windemere. He is now carefully preserving and restoring the home where Ernest Hemingway spent the happiest days of his youth.

Further Reading

Baker, Carlos. *Ernest Hemingway: A Life Story.* New York: Charles Scribner's Sons, 1969.

Cappel, Constance. *Hemingway in Michigan.* Waitsfield, Vermont: Vermont Crossroads Press, 1977.

Charlevoix *Courier,* Charlevoix, Michigan, June-September, 1915

Hemingway, Ernest. *The Nick Adams Stories.* New York: Charles Scribner's Sons, 1972.

Hemingway, Leicester H. *My Brother, Ernest Hemingway.* Cleveland and New York: World Publishing, 1961.

Mellow, James R. *Hemingway: A Life without Consequences.* Boston, New York, London: Houghton Mifflin, 1992.

Miller, Madelaine Hemingway. *Ernie.* New York: Crown, 1975. To be republished by Thunder Bay Press in 1999.

Reynolds, Michael. *The Young Hemingway.* New York and Oxford: Basil Blackwell, 1986.

Sanford, Marcelline. *At the Hemingways.* New York: Little Brown, 1961.